Cowboy

J. M. Snyder

Lulu Press
Morrisville

COWBOY

All Rights Reserved © 2008 by J.M. Snyder

Cover art © Photographer: Nolte Lourens | Agency: Dreamstime.com

The stories within are works of fiction. All events, locations, institutions, themes, persons, characters, and plots are completely fictional inventions of the author. Any resemblance to people living or deceased, actual places, or events is purely coincidental and entirely unintentional.

The entire text of this book appears on my website at jmsnyder.net in its entirety as a free download. No part of this book may be reproduced or transmitted in any form or by any means, graphic, electronic, or mechanical, including photocopying, recording, taping, or by any information storage retrieval system, without the permission in writing from the author and publisher.

Lulu Press
affiliated with Lulu Enterprises
3131 RDU Center Drive Ste 210
Morrisville, NC 27560
www.lulu.com

J.M. Snyder
P.O. Box 924
Colonial Heights, VA 23834
www.jmsnyder.net

ISBN: 978-1-4357-2090-9

Printed in the United States of America

Other trade paperbacks available by J. M. Snyder

OPERATION STARSEED

SCARRED: FOUR NOVELLAS

POWER PLAY

VINCE

IT'S ALL RELATIVE

SHORTS

TRIN

STEPPING UP TO THE PLATE

BETWEEN BROTHERS

CRUSHED

THE BONDS OF LOVE

CONFLICT OF INTEREST

FOREVER AFTER

Visit www.jmsnyder.net for a complete list of books and stories available in print and e-book formats.

part 1

Kent's Market is the only thing for miles down either side of Route 83. Rising from the midst of so much desert dirt and stubborn grass, it's an oasis of greenery and color that makes your heart stop to see it. A small picket fence corrals in the plants and flowers and vegetable carts that threaten to overflow into the dusty road, and above it all the sign, painted to look that cracked and weathered. *Kent's.*

Annuals first, right by the road, lines of pansies and wax begonias and nasturtiums, purple and red and orange in the dry air. Then the shrubbery and taller plants, hostas and hibiscus, a potted azalea or two. Old wooden workbenches line the fence, overflowing with baskets of apples and strawberries, tomatoes, green peppers, and at the back of the lot a tent stands tall, its canvas flapping in the hot breeze that blows when a car passes by. Behind the tent, a ways off to deter the shoppers who stop for fresh produce and live plants, is a low, one-story ranch house, its wooden façade as worn and beaten down as Kent's sign out front. And behind the house, hidden from view, is the field of vegetables and plants he sells.

Kent himself stands at the front of the lot every morning as the sun comes up. Hose in hand, watering the flowers, the plants, thinking things I'll never know and he doesn't wish to share. With his black jeans tucked into faded boots, a black cowboy hat pushed down low over his eyes, he looks like the epitome of what I came west to find. A solitary man, a lone cowboy, some nugget of a man's man that managed to slip sideways in time, straight off the range to me. I've always wanted a guy like that, rugged, stoic, lean and muscled and damn fine in a duster and hat. Too many westerns as a kid, my sister says. Searching for a western hero that doesn't exist, out here in the desert sun.

She never met Kent.

He's the reason women flock to our meager produce stand, out here a good ten miles from town. Sure, we advertise in the local paper, on TV, but he's the reason people driving the back road from Laredo to Abilene stop and pick up a pint of berries or a potted geranium to take home. From the road he's breath-taking in those jeans, that hat, no shirt and a tanned chest the delicious color of chestnuts in season. Strong—you can see that from your car window, how strong he is, how broad his chest and back, how muscled his arms. Narrow hips that hint at a tight ass, abs you think you saw on a NordiTrack commercial, a tiny string around his neck so Marlboro you ache for a smoke.

The women look his way and imagine a slow, shy grin curving into that tanned face, or how he'd tip the brim of his hat just so and say something John Wayne like, "Howdy, ma'am." They read about him in their historical romances, see him on the big screen—they know how cowboys like him are supposed to act and they come racing in to pick over his irises and cucumbers, nudging each other and giggling when he looks their way.

I know, I fell for it too. Only I wasn't holding out much hope when I stopped—a man like that usually doesn't go for a man like me, that's part of the reason I think I've always wanted one. But I was hitchhiking my way north and the couple who picked me up outside of Carrizo Springs were old enough to be my parents, and by the time we drove past Kent's, I was more than ready to get out. Away from the words of caution, how a young man like myself should settle down with a nice girl, how I need a job like their own son working for minimum wage in the school system over in Dallas, how their daughter would like me but I'm a bit too shiftless for their tastes…

When the missus saw Kent's bare back, as broad as the sky above, and developed a sudden craving for fresh snap peas, I made my escape. Thanked them for the ride, dug my pack out of their trunk, trotted over to the stand as if this was where I needed to be. It was—I left Jersey looking for a man like Kent. I wasn't leaving Texas without finding one.

So it was a pleasant surprise when he turned in my direction and I saw in his eyes that all the women in all the world didn't matter to him none, and when he asked if I had a place to stay, I told him no. He had an extra room in the back, if I was interested? Of course I was.

Been here ever since, going on two years now. Up close he's not so intimidating—you see the pale flesh where his pants sag a little off his hips, the small paunch that's begun to distend those abs, the flab that runs through the muscles in his arms. If the wind is right, you catch a whiff of something strong rising from him, tequila or whiskey, something pungent and tart that makes you swoon in the desert heat. There is no "ma'am" or "howdy" or shy, slow smile to brighten your day—most of the time he doesn't say two words from sun up to sundown, and in the early morning he's too hung-over to smile.

The cowboy hat, the boots, the lariat chain around his neck, it's all part of the image, the illusion, the same way his "homegrown" tomatoes are bought at the farm four miles away, or the flats of perennials purchased at the Wal-Mart in town. It's an act, a way to bring in customers and stay in business…he's a daydream out there in the sun, hose in hand, watering his plants and I fell for it so hard, I'm still dusting off my knees.

Two years. And even now when I look out from the main house, I can still see the man I thought he was, the cowboy I want him to be.

❋

I BRING HIM COFFEE, black, because that's the way he likes it. My own looks like hot cocoa, I use so much milk. Two steaming mugs, one in each hand, and my fingers start to sweat from the heat when I step out of the main house and head for the market lot. It's already close to seventy degrees outside and it's barely eight o'clock yet—by noon it'll be almost unbearable for a northern boy like me, and I'll have to retreat beneath the tent where I have a cashier's table and a fan set up, and I'll sit in the shade and watch Kent move through his plants like a mirage in the waves of heat that radiate from the desert sun. How he keeps anything green in this arid clime, I'll never know.

He's watering now, like he always is when I first come down. Setting my coffee on one of the veggie stands, I sidle up behind him and snake an arm around his waist—his skin is already damp with a fine sheen of sweat, I taste it when I kiss the back of his neck, and a bitter smell rises from him, a mix of work and alcohol and sex. "Hey babe," I purr, resting my chin on his shoulder. He's a tall man, a head taller than me, and when I lean on his shoulder, I fit perfectly beneath the brim of his cowboy hat.

This close I can see his hair, dark and plastered to his head under the hat, and he has a thin mustache that makes him look older than his thirty-two years. It makes him look more western somehow—I think of *Dallas* and *Magnum P.I.* and all those old shows I used to watch as a kid, all those shows that made me want a man like the one in my arms now.

From here I can also see his unshaven cheeks, the stubble laced with a gray fuzz that I won't point out. Instead I breathe in the whiskey that rises up from him like the sun off the road and I hold out his coffee mug where he can see it. "For you," I tell him. By noon, it'll hold more alcohol than java. He thinks I don't see when he spikes it.

Kent grunts, not quite the thanks I would like, and then shrugs out of my embrace. "Don't hang on me, Marcus," he says, his voice bleary and gruff. "It's hot out here."

No shit, I think, but I hold my tongue. I learned long ago that the best way to deal with a mood like this is to just keep quiet and let it ride itself out. Once he wakes up a bit more, shakes off the drink from last night, he'll be easier to deal with. He'll smile for the customers, at least. They're the ones that matter.

"Your coffee," I say, holding out the mug like a peace offering. He frowns at it a moment, then takes it and chugs half of it at once—good thing it wasn't scalding. I doubt he would've felt it, anyway. Shoving my hands into the pockets of my jeans, I glare at the flowers he's watering and tell him, "I have that washtub out—"

"I'm going into town in the morning," he mutters. It's his *don't nag me* tone of voice, one he's been using more and more around me. The showerhead's been busted for the past week and I'd swear he hasn't bathed since then, that's the alcohol and sweat I smell on him.

The day after the shower broke, I found an old aluminum washtub in the back of the barn, scrubbed it up and hosed it down and it's so damn pioneer that I find any excuse to strip off my clothes and sink into a lukewarm bath of suds. Out by the barn, the sun hot on my naked body, the soap drying on my skin, it's as close to heaven as I've come so far, and I can't understand why Kent won't take me up on an offer of a bath. I'd heat the water for him, on the gas grill like I do for myself—I'd wash him, *that* could be fun, maybe end up with the two of us entwined in the sparse grass, rolling through suds and water, when's the last time we did anything like that?

Heh, when have we *ever* done that?

But Kent always says no. "I'll fix the damn shower," he tells me, before I can point out that it's still clogged. "Just lay off it already, will you? Can you move back? It's hot."

As if I'm right up on him. But I do as he asks, mindful of the hose as I step back, and I watch him for a few minutes, before he can tell me to get to work. From the house this morning I leaned over the sink while the coffee brewed, watched him through the kitchen windows, told myself he's everything I've ever wanted.

But in truth he's only a shadow of the men I see in the magazine clippings my sister sends me, the models in cowboy hats and little else, Calvin Klein and Guess ads that sell what I'm hoping to find. Those cowboys don't have Kent's thick waist or his drink-rimmed eyes or his alcohol-pinked cheeks. They don't have that line where his tan stops abruptly at his hips, everything above a deep Indian red, everything below pasty and white. And they smile, in those ads. Even the cigarette ones, where the cowboy's riding hard to round up stray cattle, he always has the hint of a smile in his eyes, on his lips. Kent doesn't smile much, and he never laughs. Once I thought that was part of his appeal but now I'm not so sure.

With a sigh, he looks at me over his shoulder and says, "I'll pick up a new head when I'm in town tomorrow. I said I'd fix it—"

"Okay." I kick dirt over the hose so I won't have to meet his eyes. They're dark like his hair and bloodshot from drink, and I hate that I can't read them. I'm good at reading people but there's something closed about Kent that I just can't figure out. Maybe that's what draws me to him. Maybe there's a part of me that wants to be the one to crack through his rough exterior and find that I've been right all along, there's something deep inside of him that's exactly what I need. It's just buried, and every now and then I think I catch a glimpse of it, in a rare smile or a sudden touch, or a wink that will surprise me and take my breath away. I live for those moments, that hope.

Kent frowns at me, then cuts the hose off, downs the rest of his coffee, hands the mug to me. I take it and wrap both hands around its lingering warmth. "Marcus," he says softly. He can speak so softly when it suits him.

I look up and study his face. He needs to shave, he looks grizzled and old, and his moustache needs to be trimmed, it's getting bushy. Sometimes he lets me do that for him, after hours when it's just the two of us, and I'll sit on his lap and gently clip the hairs above his lip, or shave his cheeks in long, even strokes while he leans back in his recliner, beer close at hand, one arm draped almost negligently around my waist. We haven't done that in awhile now. I'd suggest it but I have a feeling his response would be the same as it was when I offered to bathe him. *Not right this second,* he said, exasperated. *Can't you see I'm busy?*

"I'll fix it," he tells me. He means the shower, and I nod because I know he'll fix it. He's going into town tomorrow, he'll buy the parts, we'll have a working shower by evening. When I don't answer, though, he sighs and reaches out for me, his fingers slipping behind my belt buckle to pull me close. "Come here," he says. I have no choice.

He gives me a kiss, damp and sloppy and tasting of sour whiskey, but it's his lips on mine, it's something at least. His cheeks scruff my skin and I close my eyes so he won't see the flicker of disgust in my gaze. He needs a bath, a shave, mouthwash, *something*. But it's a kiss and it's more than I was expecting, more than I could've hoped for this early in the day. If he were one of the cowboys in my daydreams, this would be when he'd whisper he loves me and I'd suggest a quick tryst out by the barn before the first customers arrive, and he'd agree.

But he doesn't say anything, just pulls away and clears his throat, asks for more coffee. And I don't offer myself to him—I just nod and grip his mug tight, head back for the house and the pot simmering on the stove. This isn't a daydream and he isn't a model in an underwear ad. My sister's right, that world doesn't exist.

This is what I got instead. As I trek back to the house, I tell myself this is enough. It's going to have to be.

✺

AFTERNOON FINDS ME BENEATH the tent, the fan stirring hot air over my denim-clad legs and a towel full of melting ice tied around my neck. When I first hooked up with Kent, I made the mistake of wearing shorts outside—came in that night with welts up and down my legs, mosquito bites and red chigger trails on my thighs, black fleas like freckles on my ankles and feet. Scratches, too, where the dust blew up against me during the day, I was raw from the heat and the dirt, and I never felt more filthy in my life.

"Now you know why cowboys wear jeans," Kent told me, and it was as close to *I told you so* as he'd ever come, but he sat with me in the bathroom as I showered, painted the chigger bites with clear nail polish to kill them, covered me in calamine lotion until I looked as pink as a newborn baby. He can be so good to me.

The customers are here now, women in bright prints swarming around the flowers like bees. They call out to Kent by name, giggling when he turns their way—how much are the petunias? And does he know a good recipe for tomatillos? And what kind of sun should these morning glories get? They don't ask me—I'm just the boy by the register, my name's not up on the sign out front and I don't have my shirt off so they can gawk over my chest, which doesn't look anything like his. I'm not tan, not buff, and if they weren't so blind, they'd see that Kent's color is more of a perpetual burn, his stomach muscles aren't as firm as I'd like them to be.

But they only see the man they came here to see, the cowboy in the black jeans and black hat who looks like he stepped off a pack of cigarettes. They sigh over him as I ring up their plants—don't they notice he's not interested? If one propositions him, he gracefully backs down, and that makes them want him all the more. *He's mine,* I want to say as I take their dingy dollars. He doesn't sleep in my bed but we have sex; that means he's with me.

A few pay him directly. I watch him stick the money in his back pocket almost absently, like he's just putting it there until he can give it to me, but somehow it never makes it into the register. He thinks I don't notice, but I know it'll be gone by the time he comes home tomorrow, spent in town on beer and pints at the local bar. I know how he is. If I mention it, though, he'll get indignant and think I don't trust him, and the air between us will be like cracked glass, threatening at any moment to shatter into an argument. So I don't say anything, and when he glances at me I look away, as if I didn't see it. Twenty bucks, maybe fifty, it's not worth the fight.

When the sky begins to grow dark and the shadow of the house stretches across the yard to reach into the tent, we close up shop. Tie down the tent flaps, cover the stands with tarp, water the plants one more time as the sun goes down. I hurry the few lingering customers along while Kent moves large, sand-filled barrels into place to block our driveway, a deterrent against anyone pulling up to browse our plants at night. Now he tips his hat, as the last couple climbs into their car, and there's a ghost of a smile on his face when they back out into the road and are gone.

Then it's just the two of us, alone, and I try not to stare at him as I count out the money in the drawer but he's beautiful in the setting sunlight, his skin the color of the arroyo, his hat pushed back to reveal his enigmatic eyes. He's been drinking since before noon, I know because I saw the empty bottles of Killian's in the trash, but it's loosened him up and he actually grins at me when he's finished watering the plants. "Good day," he tells me, meaning we were busy.

I nod and keep counting. Easily three hundred, maybe four, because he sold the rhododendron in full bloom for a pretty penny, and out in these parts plants like that are scarce, like gold or diamonds in the dust. After the tarp is down, held in place with large stones to keep the night wind from whipping it away, Kent comes up behind me, rubs a hand around my waist, over my stomach, until his thumb hooks onto my belt buckle. His fingers on my zipper arouse me despite the alcohol that rises from his pores, and when he blows on my neck, I giggle and squirm away. I'm as bad as any of those women in here earlier. "Let's cook out tonight," he says. That means he wants me to fire up the grill.

Folding the money into a deposit envelope, I ask, "Burgers?" That's about all we have right now—he'll pick up groceries tomorrow when he's in town, and put this money in the bank, and get a showerhead, I have to remind him about that. "One or two?"

He leans against me, heavy and sweaty through my thin t-shirt. "Two," he says, and I know he'll only eat one but I nod anyway, I'll cook two. Rubbing his hand against my crotch, he murmurs, "And maybe later…"

He lets the thought trail off but a thrill runs through me all the same. It's been almost a week since we've had sex, four days and three hours and I'm counting here, I am, because at twenty-eight I should be getting it more often than that. I'm in my sexual prime, right? I have to settle for my hand in the washtub because most of the time he's too drunk to get it up. But he's promising a little loving now and I've been waiting for this all damn *day*. I shove the rest of the money into the envelope, I'll count it later, and turn away from the register so fast, I almost trip over the fan and send us both to the floor. "Careful," he warns, grinning again.

"Can you tie down the tent?" I ask, turning in his one-armed embrace. This close he's intoxicating, but I don't know if it's the alcohol or the man, and right now I don't care. "Two burgers. You sure you're up for dessert?"

So he won't mistake my meaning, I poke at the front of his jeans, where he's already hard, I can feel his erection through his pants. Sometimes beer will do that to him, and tonight I'm loving George Killian and his Irish red lager if it'll get me a piece of my man. "Just make it quick," he tells me, and I'm already stumbling for the house, thank *God* we have a gas grill and I don't have to wait for charcoal to light. "I've got to leave first thing in the morning—"

"Already halfway there," I say, breaking into a jog. Vaguely I'm aware that I'm no different from the women who drive all the way out here to see him, but what's it matter? He's with me, remember? Let them dream of a cowboy in black because this one's mine.

❋

I COOK THREE BURGERS and leave one of them on the grill—I'll have it for lunch tomorrow, I know Kent well enough to know that he won't eat it tonight. He sits at the picnic bench we have out back, between the barn and the main house, and watches me through the amber bottle in his hand. More beer, at least that's all he's drinking tonight. He's not a mean drunk, not bitter or hateful or angry like some men, but the alcohol dulls his senses, makes him sleepy, makes him brood, and he'll fall asleep in his recliner, wet snores filling the house until I could smother him to shut him up. And in the morning he'll wince at the sun and the sound of my voice, and he'll tell me to keep off him, it's hot, and keep it down, I'm too loud.

But he's not a bad drunk, he doesn't hit me, doesn't yell, doesn't tell me what I'm doing wrong or how I can be someone more to him, something better. Sometimes I think if I could figure that out then maybe he wouldn't drink so much. Sometimes I wonder what kind of man he'd be without the alcohol, if he'd be like the men in my sister's magazines, the ones she tears out and sends to me with little Post-It notes stuck on the pictures. *How about this one?* she'll ask. *Have you seen one like this down there yet?*

I don't bother to write her back. What would I say? *Unfortunately...*

Kent wolfs his burger down in four bites—sometimes beer gives him an appetite, but when I ask if he wants the second burger, he shakes his head no. Instead, he gives me a smoldering look across the picnic table, and there's a fire in his eyes that the alcohol can't dim, he wants me. *Me.* Finally, he wants me. I gulp down the rest of my meal as fast as I can and take the third burger off the grill so it won't burn. I set it on my plate and pick up his when Kent stands over me, his hand curving around my ass, rubbing along the seam of my jeans. "Leave it here, Marcus," he tells me.

I nod, suddenly famished for him. "I'll get it afterwards," I say, my voice cracking like the desert ground. His fingers fumble between my legs and I lean on the table, arch up into his hand, moan at his touch. From the corner of my eye I see his belt already unbuckled, his other hand rubbing at the front of his jeans. I hope we at least make it inside.

We do, but just barely. He drops his pants the minute the screen door slams shut behind him, and I can't seem to get my belt to work, I want it undone, I want it open and I want my pants gone *now*. Kent's already working himself hard, another few minutes and we'll miss this, it'll end in a rush of thin, beer-laced cum on his hand and the floor and I'll be out of luck.

Somehow I manage to get my belt loose enough to shuck my jeans down my narrow hips, and my boxers follow suit, I don't think we're even going to make it as far as my bedroom because he won't be able to get it up again if we miss this now. "Kent," I sob, I want him so bad, it's been too long and I want someone in me, holding me, loving me, *anyone* at this point. "Babe, do you think—"

That's as far as I get to asking if he wants to hold on until we get to my room, because he touches me and that's it, that's all I really wanted, his hand on me in places that quiver for another's touch. His hands are large, calloused, rough, but they turn me on when he cups my balls, strokes my hard shaft, caresses the smooth skin of my ass. He eases inside of me, one finger, two, and then he presses his thick cock in, I swear it's as rough and large and calloused as those hands.

I have to grip the back of the recliner and spread my legs to get him all the way in, and the way I'm standing makes me giggle breathlessly. We never do it lying down. Sex is standing up in this house, and it's usually against the foot of my bed but this in the living room, that's new. It makes me think maybe we're not as settled into routine as I feared. God, if any customers pulled up now and dared to creep around the back of the house, they'd get an eyeful through the screen door. Kent shoving into me as I lean over the recliner, his breath coming in quick huffs that reek of beer, his dark hands on my hips and his white ass probably gleaming in the dusk. He's that pale below his waist. The image makes me laugh as he pushes further into me. "What?" he wants to know.

It comes out like a grunt, and his fingers dig into my skin. I arch back into him and close my eyes, savor the fullness inside, my muscles working to hold him in even as he tries to pull back out. "Assume the position," I say, just to be silly. I can *be* silly right now if I want to—I'm finally getting him, he's finally mine.

He's a selfish lover, only works for himself and when he's done, he thinks I should be, too. Not one for foreplay, doesn't like sucking or kissing or hugging or anything like that. No, just a fuck for him, just sex, and it's always me on the receiving end because he says it just doesn't do anything for him to get it up the ass. He can be crude when he's sober, and it makes me laugh because he's so quiet, you don't expect it from him. The first few times we had sex, he would pull out just as he started to come and I'd end up with his juices trickling down my ass cheeks, hot and wet and so damn nasty that it was enough to get me off, as well.

Only now I know he pulls out because he *can't* come, that's the beer in him, it makes him hard and he can go all night long if he wants, but there's no release. He thinks he's slick when he moans my name and bucks into me ten, fifteen minutes later, and suddenly he's finished. What the—? I look over my shoulder and he's already tucking himself back into his jeans. One hand is fisted like he came in it, but I know he didn't. I know he can't. "Kent," I sigh. I don't bother to pull up my own pants. I'm not done yet.

"You're good," he tells me, like that's a consolation. It doesn't make my dick any less hard, it doesn't make the dull throb that has settled into my balls go away. With a slap on my ass, he heads for the kitchen and I hear running water when he turns on the sink to wash his hand off. Does the pretense go that far? Does he *think* he's gotten off from this?

I stand there, naked, clutching the back of the recliner, and I look at him incredulously when he comes into the room. "Babe," I start. I'm still looking for more.

He doesn't like it when I call him that. He says it always sounds like I'm whining, *babe,* like I'm trying to wheedle something out of him. "Don't start with me, Marcus," he says, weary. "I'm tired. I can't keep it up all night like you—"

"All night?" I ask. Who's he kidding? We're talking barely a half hour here. Is it so bad to not want such a rush job? From my *lover,* no less?

"I've got to get up early in the morning," he tells me as he heads down the hall to his room. When I start to say something else, he holds up one hand to stop me. "A showerhead, I know. I'll pick it up."

I'd like to pick *this* up, where we were a few minutes ago. My hand trails down my stomach almost absently, heading for the erection that still stands up from the patch of blonde hair at my crotch as if refusing to believe we're through. That's it. And he called this *dessert*? Heh, this was a spoonful of whipped cream, one strawberry, maybe a bite of cake, nothing more than a mouthful, if that. Neither of us got off on it, despite whatever lies he wants to tell himself. I'm aching here and I know he held nothing in his hand, nothing at all.

Down the hall his door closes softly, almost like an apology, and I'm left with my dick in hand, staring around myself in disbelief. I got worked up for this? I cooked him burgers on the grill, two of them, for *this*? My sex life with him is like rain in the desert, a scarce occurrence that is barely-there and brief when it does happens. And those women earlier, our customers, they seriously think they want in on that?

Disgusted, I kick my pants off from my ankles and head for my own room, my long t-shirt covering my ass and cock and the hand that works at my crotch. Beneath my bed is a folder of all the magazine clippings my sister's sent, all those underwear and cigarette and cologne ads, all those cowboys in their Stetson hats and bolo ties, flannel shirts, spurs and chaps. I kneel on my bed, the folder open in front of me, and my own hand has to squeeze and knead as I flip through the pictures, imaging those boys with me. I picture their lips on my skin, their hands on me, their fingers doing the delicious things I have to do myself while Kent sleeps off the booze in the room next door.

Finally I come in an embarrassed spurt that slicks my hand and belly and I wipe myself clean with my shirt before putting the folder carefully

Cowboy

away. Those are my men in there, those are my boys, not the snoring cowboy who stuck it to me tonight.

Until tomorrow, of course, when I see him from the window, his skin bronzed by the sun. If only he could love me *then,* at that moment, when he's everything I want him to be and more. If only *that* man came to me after the market closes. That man has to be in him somewhere, right? That man is who I love about him, right?

❋

LATER, WHEN I REMEMBER the plates on the table outside, I move through the house quietly so I won't wake Kent, unashamed of my nakedness. In the living room, I pull on my boxers and leave the jeans on the floor, then push through the screen door out into the cool night. It's almost cold out here—the temperature drops once the sun goes down—and I hurry across the stony ground, telling myself I don't feel the gravel biting into my feet. The grill is cold now and I close its cover, working quickly because it's chilly and I'm wearing next to nothing. It's odd how a body grows used to things, after living with them for so long. In Jersey, this would've been a balmy summer night, I would've thought nothing of running down to the beach in shorts thinner than these boxers I have on now. But after two years I'm almost shivering here, and I bet it's not below sixty degrees. How did I ever survive before?

The plates are where I left them, but the bag of chips is gone, the extra burger, gone. I look beneath the table, under the benches, around the darkened yard for as far as I can see, but they've simply vanished. The scarce dirt is unmarked, no prints from a coyote or bobcat or weasel, and there aren't any feathers scattered around from vultures, but that doesn't mean anything. The worse thing is that whatever ate the burger and made off with the chips will probably come back tomorrow looking for more, and Kent hates animals prowling around his garden, he'll take the gun down from over the stove and heaven help us then. He's not a good shot when he's *not* drunk, and I'd hate to see him when he's been hitting the booze.

I gather up the plates, the cups, the tongs I used to turn the burgers on the grill, and head for the house. I won't mention it, then. Maybe ask him to pick up some poison in town tomorrow, tell him we have rats, I'll take care of it myself. He doesn't need to know anything more than that.

❋

I WAKE TO THE slap of the screen door—Kent leaving, and a glance at the clock beside my bed shows that it's not even six AM yet. I pull the blankets over my head and wish the warmth that surrounds me wasn't just my own. Some mornings I would give anything to have the memory of his body lingering next to me. But he goes to bed before I do, wakes up too damn early, tells me that he likes a separate room because it keeps me from rousing him when I turn in at night. The explanation doesn't make my own bed any less lonely.

I'm almost back to sleep when I hear tires spin to a stop in front of the house, the truck door slam shut, heavy boots on the porch and then he's back inside, muttering to himself because he's forgotten something. Through half-closed eyes I watch the hallway beyond my open door. He troops by, stomping in those cowboy boots like he doesn't care if he wakes me or not, and the glimpse I get of his tan arms, his bare chest, his black hat and jeans, it makes me catch my breath.

Come here, I want to say—I would if I thought he would listen, if I thought he would let me soothe away the anger that's bunched his brows together, let me make everything alright. I hear him in the bathroom, fiddling with the showerhead—something hits the tiled floor, he curses and throws something else down, I'm going to have to clean that up when he leaves. Then he passes my room again, heading for the door and his truck outside, and whatever chance I might have had to convince him to join me has passed.

So I wait. Until the sound of the wheels fade away in the morning sun, until the house has settled around me like a troubled pond growing still, until the clock reads a little before seven and I just can't stay in the bed any longer. In the bathroom I find the small aluminum tubing that holds the showerhead in place, it's tossed to the floor of the stall—no tub for Kent. Just a shower stall, a toilet, a sink so battered and dingy that I can never get it clean. The shower rod is askew, the curtain pulled free from a few of its fastenings.

He was probably pissed to all hell that he left without the head this morning, the one thing he's going into town to get. I should've been up to remind him, but then he would've acted like forgetting it was *my* fault, and he'd be grumpy and ill-tempered for days. I won't mention that I know he came back for it. Not if I hope for a little loving when he returns.

Like last night, I think sourly. Heh, that wasn't loving, that was a few good thrusts and then poof, nothing. I shouldn't put up with that shit. I need more than that to survive.

I pull on jeans and a t-shirt, a pair of cowboy boots because that's all we wear around here, a thin flannel shirt that covers my arms. But as I tug my blankets onto my bed, I catch a whiff of rank sex, alcohol, sweat, Kent on me, that man *needs* to bathe. When he gets that showerhead installed, I'm throwing his lily-white ass in the stall myself. We'll do it in the shower if we have to, anything to get him cleaned up. Is that what those boys in the ads smell like? That raw mix of man and beast? I have to get it off of me.

The washtub's out in the barn. This early, I can get a quick bath in before the first customers arrive—not that I'm expecting many, because Kent's not here to pimp in the midst of his Eden, no one's going to see me from the road and stop with a sudden taste for berries. But a few regulars will come by, a few cars passing will stop, we'll do a meager business, and I'd much rather be fully dressed and waiting by the register when the first car pulls into our lot than crammed naked into that tiny tin tub out back. A bath, breakfast, then I'll open shop. It won't be at Kent's ungodly hour, but I can make it before eight, at least.

As I push through the screen door, I look around the backyard, which is nothing more than a run of stunted grass and cobbled dirt between here and our barn. Away to the right I can just barely see the road glistening in the already hot morning sun, and to the left our fields start, row after row of plants and vegetables that Kent somehow manages to eke from this soil. Remembering the lost burger last night, I eye the garden rows warily, sure that something's hidden among the leaves, watching me, waiting for more food. It's quiet, too quiet, but it's also the heart of Texas and I just might be the only living thing around for miles, I can't expect more than the silent line of crows that sit like black dots on the telephone wires lining the road.

Crossing the yard, I notice that the barn door is ajar. I'm fairly certain I didn't leave it that way—I *always* close it when I'm done, after the time a possum was hit on the road and managed to drag itself into our loft. I found it dead the next morning, blood everywhere, the heat making me swoon from the stench, and I stumbled from the barn gagging as Kent watched with impassive eyes. "Road kill," was all he said, but he took the rake and cleaned out the hay, disposed of the carcass, didn't mention my moment of weakness—I can't help but love him for that. Since then, I make sure to pull the barn door tight behind me whenever I'm through in there, latch the rope toggle lock across the doors, check it before I go inside. I know I didn't leave that door open last night.

A coyote then? The rope isn't chewed, though, I don't know how an animal could get inside. *Kent did it,* I tell myself, easing the door open as I peer in where it's dark and cool and silent. *This morning, whatever reason, he came in the barn for something and forgot to latch it closed, that's all and you know it.* The *rope's intact and he's probably hung-over so you know he wasn't thinking when he left. He forgot the showerhead, didn't he?* True. So he forgot to latch down the barn, too. In the dirt beneath my boots are shoe prints—no animal paws, no blood. He forgot to latch the door, is all.

The hinges creak as I push the door open further—I wince at the sound, impossibly loud in the quiet dawn, and slip inside the barn. My heart is hammering in my ears. Maybe Kent did open the door this morning, but who's to say something didn't slip in after he left? Coyotes are bad out this way. Kent used to keep chickens but he couldn't stop the damn dogs from getting at them, and even now one or two will prowl the old coop, out at the far edge of the field.

Sometimes when he's *really* drunk, off the tequila usually, he'll take his gun down from the wall and head out that way, claim he'll put a stop to those rascals once and for all, and I swear one day he's going to come back with a hole shot in his foot, he's foolish when he gets too far into the bottle. But what if those coyotes are hanging around now? What if one of them slipped into the barn after the truck left, and it's watching me from the loft, or the empty horse stall, or the bundles of hay piled against the wall, just waiting for a chance to jump me?

A shaft of sunlight slants through the partially open door, slicing into the darkness, and I try to look everywhere at once. Jesus, but I can get worked up over stupid shit, and in another few minutes when that washtub's outside and I'm filling it with the hose, I'll laugh away my fears, but right now, right here, they're palpable and real and pressing in on me like the musty scent of hay that tickles my nose, the faint stirring of bats in the rafters. The tub's against the horse stall, the sunlight cuts across it with a silver promise, two steps and I'll reach it and I'll turn and run, no one's here to see me, coyote or no—

There's a leg in the horse stall.

A human leg, denim clad, ending in a strong, bare, pale foot. For an instant I think it's Kent but he's gone and the jeans are a faded blue like the sky above, not his signature black. I think of the possum, the blood that time, staining the hay. I wonder if coyotes will drag a body to hide it. I wonder if coyotes attack humans and what the hell am I going to do if there's a big-ass dog sitting on a dead hitchhiker in that stall? Where the hell is Kent when I need him?

Before I can take a step in either direction, the leg moves, I hear the rustle of hay, the slight moan of someone asleep. *Asleep.* Relief floods through me, *asleep.* Cautiously I cross the barn, lean on the washtub as I peer over the side of the stall, and on the hay spread out along the floor lies a man. A boy, really, all angles, much thinner than Kent and slimmer than me. A cowboy hat hides his face and he huddles into his shirt, his knees pulled up to his chest, his jeans ragged around the ankles and shiny with wear across his butt. Sneakers half-hidden in the hay, socks tucked in them to keep out scorpions and snakes, and the missing bag of chips rolled shut against them. A boy.

As I watch, he takes a shuddery breath, hugs himself tight, mutters something and falls silent. Still asleep. Quietly I edge around the washtub and into the stall, tiptoeing so my boot heels don't wake him. He's long and thin, and there's something about him that makes me think he's been on the road awhile. I have pictures of boys like this, their belongings tied in a bandanna slung over one shoulder, shirts open to show bare chests beneath, the band of their briefs snug at their waists while their jeans droop down, thumb out to hitch a ride. I've dreamed of boys like this, with these narrow legs, these slim hips, these sinewy arms holding me tight. He has thick ankles, I like that, and long toes that I want to thread my fingers through. Nice feet. I like that a lot.

And nice hands, I can see the one gripping his elbow where his arms are crossed—long fingers, an artist's hands, even nails despite the dirt rimmed beneath them. Dusky skin, a farmer's tan, nothing like what Kent has but darker than me. He probably has dark hair, then, and dark eyes, hidden beneath that cowboy hat. Reaching out, I pick up the brim of the hat, just to see...

Purple eyes like pansies stare back at me.

Startled, I drop the hat and skid back into the corner of the stall, heart racing. Holy *fuck,* he's not asleep—

Like an animal waiting to pounce, he's up, scrambling for his sneakers as he scurries for the door. "Wait!" I call out. Those eyes burn in my head, the deep color of violets in bloom, *purple.* "No, wait, don't go—"

He stops and sulks back against the opposite end of the stall, hat pulled low to hide those amazing eyes and shoes hugged to his chest like a shield. "Wait," I say again, gently, oh so gently. *Please,* I pray, holding one hand out towards him. *Please don't run away.* "It's okay," I murmur. He stares at me balefully and my hand closes into a useless fist before dropping to the hay. "It's okay."

He glances at the door and sniffles, rubs his feet together with a dry, soughing sound that makes me think of limbs lying twined together in bed. I want to say something to make him come closer so I can see his eyes again. "It's okay," I tell him. "Believe me. I'm not going to hurt you."

"You snuck up on me," he mutters. He sounds like a little kid. I can hear the pout in his voice.

"I didn't mean to." I start towards him but he moves for the door again, so I stop and he does, too. "What's your name, boy?"

For a moment I don't think he'll answer. He glares at me like I'm evil, waking him like I did, as if this isn't my barn but his and I'm the trespasser here, not him. But then he sniffs again, rubs his nose so hard that I think he'll rub it off, and he mumbles, "Luke. And I'm not a boy."

Bullshit, I think, but I'll bite. "How old are you, Luke?" I ask. I wonder if Luke's his real name.

"Twenty." He pushes the hat back and I catch a glimpse of light brown hair cut short across his forehead before I'm lost in his eyes again. Royal and deep, the color of kings. Purple. Beneath them his nose is a little too big for his face, his mouth a little too wide, his cheeks pinked with excitement or fear and his lips full and red and pretty like a girl's. Kissable lips. Suddenly I want to kiss him. "Who are you?" he wants to know.

"Marcus."

I'm staring at his lips, I know I am, and I shouldn't because I have a lover, I have Kent, I don't need to be wanting for this boy. It's one thing to ache for the guys in the magazine ads because they're not *real,* they're models and I'm in no danger of actually meeting up with them...but these eyes watching me, this boy, *he's* real, he's here, watching me because I can't stop looking at him, and I'll be damned if he's a day over seventeen. Twenty my ass. He's jailbait, plain and simple, and he's on the run from someone, his folks or the law, boys like him don't just hole up in a barn for the night for the hell of it. I have Kent—

"Why are you sleeping here?" I ask.

He shrugs. "Just passing through," he whispers. Picking at the laces on his sneakers, he frowns and doesn't look at me when he asks, "Are you gonna tell him?"

"Who?"

"That guy." Luke nods at the door, then glances at the bag of potato chips and sighs. "The one you live with? I saw you two last night. Him."

"Kent." When I say the name he looks at me and nods, and I shake my head. "He's gone into town." I see the way he eyes the chips again and ask, "Are you hungry?"

I get an indifferent shrug in reply. "I can make you something to eat," I start, rising to my feet, but he skitters against the wall and I stop, half-erect. "It's okay," I tell him. "I'm not going to hurt you, it's okay." At the disbelief in his eyes, I add, "Kent's gone all day. I can make you some eggs, how's that sound?" I creep closer—he watches me, wary, but doesn't bolt this time. He's waiting to see what I'm going to do. I'm curious about that one myself. When Kent finds him…I won't think of that. I keep talking as I move closer. "And some toast," I say, yes, toast is good. "I have some juice, fresh fruit, too. What do you say we take this inside, okay? I'll fix up something for us to eat. You're hungry, aren't you?"

His gaze shifts from my face to the chips, then back to me again, and this time the fear is gone, his eyes lighten and his lower lip trembles as he nods. "A little," he tells me. "All I've had was that burger last night."

Another step and I'm in the middle of the hay, still tamped down where he slept. "I figured that," I say, giving him a bright grin that he doesn't return. I'd love to see him smile. Holding my hand out, I prompt, "Come on, Luke. Breakfast, then." When he looks at my offered hand and doesn't take it immediately, I whisper, "I'm just as scared as you, kid, trust me. I thought you were dead—"

Now he laughs, and his smile is everything I thought it would be, wide and beautiful, and his laughter fills the barn until the bats above flap their wings in disgust. "I did!" I laugh, too, and he lets me take his elbow, help him to his feet. His arm feels thin and strong in my hand, delicate like an eagle's wing. "I found a possum in here once," I tell him, just to fill the silence between us. "And I saw your legs and was like oh please Jesus, don't let him be dead, you know? The last thing I need is a dead body in the barn and Kent in town. What the hell would I do then?"

Luke lets me lead him to the door and the bright sunshine beyond. "He your partner or something?" he asks, holding his sneakers close to his chest. I notice the gravel doesn't seem to bother him as we cross the yard and head for the house.

The way he says *partner* makes me wonder if he means what I think of when I say the word. "This is his place," I say carefully. In my mind I hear Luke's voice, *I saw you two last night,* and then, *All I've had was that burger…*did he see us through the open screen door? Me gripping the recliner, Kent thrusting into me, did he *see* that? "He runs the produce stand," I tell Luke, "and tends to the fields. I sort of do everything else." *And sometimes we fuck,* I add silently. *Not as often as I'd like, and God knows it's not much.*

But I don't tell him *that*.

✻

HE EATS LIKE HE hasn't had food in days—leaning over the plate, shoveling eggs and toast and pancakes into his mouth as he looks around the kitchen with wide eyes. Every time those purple depths pass over me, flames of desire lick across my groin. I've never seen eyes like his, *ever,* and I find myself wondering what they look like first thing in the morning or last thing at night. Without his hat, I see that his hair is short and an almost mousy brown, bleached colorless at the top from long days in the sun, but it's getting shaggy near the back, curling over his collar and around his earlobes. Luke. I like that name. As he eats, I ask, "How old are you really?" When he looks up at me, surprised, I grin. "Twenty? You're joking."

"In two months," he says, indignant. Swallowing another mouthful of food, he tells me, "It's soon enough. How old are you?"

I laugh—he shifts the conversation away from himself so easily. "How old do you think I am?" I ask, suddenly coy. He makes me feel young and flirty again. God, has it been so long since a boy's looked at me the way he does, with such openness in his face, such unabashed interest? Or am I just so unused to kindness that I'm reading too much into him?

He shrugs and turns back to his plate. "Twenty-three," he declares, and I have to laugh again. With a shy smile, he asks, "What?"

I look *much* older than twenty-three. I know, I've seen myself in the mirror. Some days I look ancient. "You're just saying that to be nice," I say, and that makes him laugh. "I'm not that young."

Eating his eggs, he shrugs again. "You could be," he tells me. "You're not as old as your friend."

"Kent." I've noticed Luke won't say his name. "He's only thirty-two."

Another shrug, like that's no concern of his. "He looks like an old fart," he says, and so nonchalantly that I burst out laughing, I can't help it. "What?" Luke asks, confused. "He does. Drinks like a fish and can't fuck worth a damn—" My laughter dries up instantly and he ducks his head to keep from meeting my gaze. "Sorry," he mumbles. "I didn't mean that."

My voice sounds like it comes from miles away when I reply, "It's okay." It's the truth, isn't it? And I don't know what hurts worse, hearing the words out loud or knowing that it took a stranger to point them out to me. *Can't fuck worth a damn...*softly, I whisper, "I'm twenty-eight."

Luke nods, his purple eyes looking everywhere but at me as he finishes his breakfast. "That's not old at all," he says. Spearing a strawberry with his fork, he rolls the fruit in the sugar bowl and then holds it out to me. "You still hungry? Open up."

My mouth pops open on its own, and I watch his face as he guides the fork towards me, his eyes never leaving the strawberry perched on the tines. When the fruit touches my lips I taste sweet sugar, cool juices, and a heady, ripe scent envelops me. He still watches the fork as I close my mouth over it and bite off the strawberry, then he pulls it through my lips slowly. His eyes are dark in the overhead light, the color of deep bruises, and his lips are parted slightly, so damn luscious and I want to taste *him,* I have a feeling he'll be a hundred times sweeter than the strawberry, a hundred times juicier and more ripe. "You want some more?" he asks, his voice throaty and low, and part of me knows he's not talking about the fruit anymore.

Outside, a car horn toots, spoiling the moment. *Kent.* I rise from the table a little too fast and almost knock my chair out from under me. *He's back,* I think, even as I hurry around the table to the door, and I know that's not right, he won't be back for hours. But what am I doing here? Flirting with this boy I hardly know like I'm single again and this isn't my lover's kitchen. "Marcus?" Luke asks, concerned. "Is it—"

"No." It's a customer, an older man helping his wife from the car, a couple of kids climbing out of the back seat. I push open the screen door and wave. "Be right there!" I holler, my voice carrying across the flat land easily. The man nods and I let the screen door slam shut behind me. "Just some customers," I tell Luke as I gather the dishes up from the table. "I've got to get to work but you're welcome to stay if you want."

"Why?" he asks. I reach for his plate but he stops me with a hand on my wrist. I look at him and he's staring up at me, those eyes like faceted jewels in his face, that beautiful, that precious. Before I can ask *why what?*, he wants to know, "Why are you so nice to me? If it'll get you in trouble with your friend…"

"It won't," I assure him. Sure, Kent will be mad, but we're not doing anything here, right? Luke will move on in a day or two, and I hate myself but I already know I'll think of him the next time Kent sticks it to me. I'll remember those eyes, these hands, this brief touch and that bit with the strawberry, and I won't need my folder of ads to get off then. I'll have *this.*

But Luke persists. "I can pay you," he tells me. "If you want."

"I don't need any money," I say. I'm sure he only has a handful of bills, if that.

This time when I try for the plate, he holds me tight, and his fingers stroke along the tender spot below my thumb. "I don't mean money," he whispers. I look into his dark eyes and see the same thoughts that swirl through my own mind, images of the two of us naked in the hay, or rolling beneath the covers of my bed, or right here against the table and that makes my throat swell shut with an unbidden lust. He wants me, and in his eyes I see the promise of release, a fulfillment I haven't had in years, a completion that would leave us both satiated and—

Kent.

I shake my head, clearing the images away. "No, really," I say, and he lets go of my wrist, lets me take his plate. "I'm with...I mean, I can't—"

"Do you love him?" Luke wants to know.

I turn towards the sink as I answer so I won't have to see disappointment cloud his eyes. Do I love Kent? The man I see when I watch him from the window? The man I want when I want him? "Yes."

For a moment I think that's it. I turn on the faucet, begin to fill the sink, and from the window I watch the man and his wife, threading through the daisies and mums to get to the vegetable stands. One of the kids, a little boy, picks a potted daffodil and hands the flower to the woman, who scolds him until he sticks the stem back into the soil, as if it will grow again. From behind me, Luke clears his throat and asks, "Then why are you like this to me?"

He means flirtatious. He means so damn nice. *I don't know,* I should say. *You look like what I came west to find,* I could tell him, but he doesn't need to know that. *You're everything I want in a boy, and I may love Kent but right this instant I want to love you. I want to hold you and thrust into you and kiss you, and I think maybe it'll be more than sex, even though we just met. You're not too drunk to come and you're young enough to keep up with me, I could use something like you to remind me how great two men can be together. I think with you, sex could be phenomenal and real once again.* I can't say *that*. Just say that I'm doing the Good Samaritan routine, then, simply being neighborly, isn't that what the west is all about?

But when I open my mouth, I surprise myself by saying, "I like your eyes. They're very pretty."

His only response is another question. "Does he love you?"

Startled, I drop the dishes into the sink, the clank of porcelain on stainless steel muffled beneath the rushing water from the spigot. *Does he love you?*

I don't reply because I don't know the answer to that.

❋

BEFORE HE LEFT THIS morning, Kent unfurled the tent flaps, removed the tarps from the vegetable stands, and watered everything down. He's all about watering those plants, he'd do it all day long if the customers didn't bother him. The hose is still wound through the make-shift aisles, between plants and over stones, and when Luke wants to know if there's anything he can do to help out, the first thing I ask is if he'll coil the hose back up. I don't need someone tripping over it and suing me because they didn't see the damn thing.

We get a meager turnout today—half the women who stop come

straight up to the register beneath the tent to ask me where Kent is. "In town," I tell them, and their eyes light up like they're actually going to go looking for him when they leave here. *Check the bars,* I should say. I'm sure he's already spent that twenty in his pocket, and I just hope he had enough sense to make the deposit before he started hitting the bottles or he'll go through that money, too.

As I fan myself with a receipt book, I watch Luke—he moves the way I wish Kent would, fluid and quick, and when he's done putting away the hose, he gets out a watering can, starts walking around the small lot, pinching dead leaves and wetting the wilting flowers. Sometime before noon, it gets too hot for him and he slips out of his shirt, and his chest is slim and young and muscled, what I want Kent's to be. His battered cowboy hat is brown, not black, and his worn jeans match the cloudless sky, but from where I sit, he's just as beautiful as Kent is when he's moving through his greenery.

More so, if that's possible, because Luke's skin isn't burnt and when he passes by me, a miasma of alcohol and sweat doesn't follow behind him, and every single time he looks at me, I don't bother to look away. I'm staring at him, I know I am, but in the shade of the tent I can pretend he doesn't notice, and from this distance I can tell myself that's not a hint of a smile I see on his face, in his eyes. I'm just looking, is all. There's nothing wrong with that.

And there's plenty to look at, too—Luke is easy on the eyes, soothing the way a watercolor painting is, all soft strokes and muted colors, familiar even if you've never seen it before just because it makes you relax. He makes me feel like I've known him forever, with his quick laugh and his regal eyes. I've seen his wide mouth and narrow hips in dreams, I've tasted every inch of that darkened flesh while I slept, and by the time the last customer leaves the lot a little after five, I've already made love to him a million times in my mind, in a million positions. Tonight when I lie down alone, I'll touch myself and think of him.

The choppy sounds from the customer's motor fade away in the late afternoon sun as I total out the register and start to count the money we've made. Not much—not as much as we get when Ken's here, that's for sure—but Luke had his fair share of interested women today, especially once that shirt came off. I wasn't the only one watching him. I saw one lady go so far as to slip her hand into his back pocket, but he stepped away blithely enough. It's because he's so young, I tell myself, counting out the bills. If he were older, if he were *Kent,* she would've kept her damn hands to herself.

I hear footsteps crunch over gravel and look up as Luke approaches.

Sweat glistens on his skin like jewels, flashing in the sunlight for a brief second, but then he's in the shade of the tent and his skin is draped in shadow. He rubs at the back of his neck with a damp towel, sighs as he hops up on the table beside the register. Beside me.

This close, the smell of him is almost overwhelming. Not alcohol like Kent's stench, not dirty or rancid or old, but something deeper, something natural and rugged and intoxicating, it stirs my groin and makes my fingers tremble with want. *This* is what that lady felt, I think, as I try to concentrate on the money, but I've already lost count. She caught a whiff of this musky scent and couldn't *stop* herself from touching him.

I don't know how I manage to keep from doing that myself.

"You want me to water again?" he asks, watching me thumb through the bills. I'm sure he knows I want him—it's in the way I can't meet his amethyst gaze, the way I shift from foot to foot to keep from moving closer. I shake my head in reply. I don't even trust myself to speak. Reaching out, he touches my wrist, and his fingers sear my flesh like the summer sun. "You okay?" he wants to know.

"Fine," I tell him, but my throat is dry and my voice parched, and the only thing that could soothe my thirst is him. *Kent,* I remind myself, but right at this moment, with this hand on mine? I can't recall the contours of my lover's face, the feel of his body, and I don't quite remember what the fuss over him is all about.

Watching me, Luke starts to rub his thumb across my wrist, just above the light hair on my arm. It's a soft touch, gentle, but it fills me with a sudden lust that trembles my hands and weakens my knees. I want to lie him down on this table and tear into him, his tender touch does that to me. I should tell him to stop but I can't find the words, and just as I'm about to pull away, he lets go. "I'm a mess," he says, slapping at his jeans. A fine dust rises from the denim. "God, what I wouldn't give for a shower."

"I hate to have to tell you this," I laugh, at ease now that he's not touching me and I can pretend that I don't want him to, "but our showerhead's been broke for awhile now. That's one of the things on Kent's list to pick up in town today."

With a slight frown, Luke asks, "So I have to wait for him to get back before I can get cleaned up? I could take the hose—"

"There's a washtub," I say. And I should stop now, I see the way his eyes light up, but before I know it, the words are tumbling out on their own. "I can fix you a bath, if you want."

Tell me you can do it yourself, I pray. All those daydreams of me washing my lover in that tub flood through me, only it's not Kent I see now but

Cowboy 23

Luke, and I give up all pretense of counting the cash, I just cram it into the bank bag, the images of Luke and me rolling on wet grass with suds drying on our naked skin too much to take. *Say thanks but you can get it, say you don't need my help, say—*

"Would you?"

Eagerness tints his voice and when I look into his deep eyes, I see a hope blossom that I know I put there. I'm leading him on, aren't I? What happens when Kent comes back and I have to tell this boy that I'm just flirting here, I don't mean anything by it?

I don't, do I?

It sounds like somebody else who replies, "Sure. I don't mind."

❋

HE GETS THE TUB for me from the barn—it's not so heavy when it's empty but it's awkward and makes a hollow *thud* every time it hits his legs as he walks. "Over here," I say, pointing out a spot by the side of the barn, where the sun hits the grass as it slants down in the sky. He does as I say, then stands back as I angle the hose into the tub. Water splashes against the aluminum, loud like rain on a tin roof, and Luke retreats to the picnic table to watch.

From the corner of my eye I see him unlace his sneakers, pull them and his socks off, and because I figure the jeans are next, I turn my back to him. I *don't* need to see him naked, no matter how much the thought thrills me. Over the sound of the water I call out, "Thanks for helping me today."

"No problem," Luke replies as he comes to stand beside me. I glance at him just as he's stretching, his chest smooth and his arms reaching for the sky, his jeans slipping a little low on his hips to show the hint of underwear, more skin, nothing pasty like Kent's untanned regions but all the same color, a luscious blend of light golden brown that reminds me of how I take my coffee.

I could take him. It'd be so easy and I know he wants me to, it's in the way he stands so close to me, the way his elbow brushes my arm when he plants his hands on his hips and stares into the foaming water. "It's the least I can do," he says, talking about helping me run the lot today. He curls his toes in the grass, picks at the blades, tears them out of the ground and lets them fall as he pulls at more, and every time he wobbles unsteadily, he bumps against me. That can't be on purpose, can it?

"I have nothing else to do," he's telling me, but I can't focus on the words, all I hear is the sound of his voice. "I guess I should get going after this? Maybe. If you're friend's coming back. I don't think he'll like me here."

I don't ask *why not?* or point out that we're doing nothing wrong because the tension is there between us, the desire is real, and even if we're not doing anything at all, that doesn't change the fact that I *want* to, and that frightens me. Yes, better that he's not here when Kent comes home. "Where are you headed?" I ask.

The tub's almost full now, mountains of suds foaming up to the lip, and the minute I turn off this water, he'll strip down beside me and I don't know if I can handle that. I don't know if I trust myself to look away. Better to think of him leaving, no matter how much I don't want to see him go. Better for us *both* if we don't make this into something more.

He shrugs. "Don't know," he mutters.

"No plans?" I want to know. When he shakes his head, I let up on the nozzle and look at him closely. He avoids my gaze, stares at the tub and sniffs in that way he has that makes him look like a little boy trying not to cry. I still can't quite believe he's almost twenty. Gently, I ask, "Where are you from, Luke?"

He shrugs again. "Nowhere," he whispers, and this time I don't think that sniffle is forced. His eyes waver with sudden tears, the purple an almost midnight shade in the setting sun. "There's no one back there looking for me," he says, so softly that I cut off the hose just to hear him speak. "Don't worry, Marcus, I'm not on the run or nothing. My momma died when I was real little—I never knew her, don't remember her much. My dad…"

With a bitter laugh, he wipes at his mouth with the back of his hand as if trying to rid himself of a bad taste. "Caught me out back with a boy when I was twelve. What did we know? Just two kids jerking off, you know? He laid into my ass then, Jesus. I swear I didn't sit for days."

I smile sadly and Luke shakes his head. "He's like your friend, only he's mean when he's drunk, real mean."

"Kent's not mean," I tell him. "He's just…he gets pissy but it's nothing like hitting and screaming and shit. Mostly he just sulks and sleeps it off." *And he can't fuck,* I add silently.

Luke rubs at his nose again and sighs. "My dad's mean. When I was fifteen, I rode around with a bad crowd, older kids mostly, we'd go into San Angelo for the day to hang out at the mall. Nothing else to do, you how that is." I nod and he continues. "The guy with the car, he was older than me, a good four years at least, but he was cute and God, could he kiss. We weren't exclusive but it was damn near love in my eyes. He'd keep his arm around my waist, kiss on me when he felt like it, tell me sexy things just so I'd giggle and blush. Fifteen, mind you."

I nod again—I remember that time. I lived in Jersey still, by the shore, and I'd flirt with any guy in a Speedo who looked my way. First time I had sex was under the boardwalk at midway that year, an older guy from Canada who was ten years my senior, but he had a tight ass and he got into my swim trunks as easily as salt water. I'm about to laugh and tell Luke I remember fifteen *all* too well, and I'll wink at him because it's a good memory and now as I think back, it's him I see over my shoulder, thrusting into me with a guttural moan.

Before I can say anything, I catch a glimpse of Luke's damp eyes and the words dissolve in my throat. "My dad was at the mall that day," he whispers. "I didn't know. When I got home, he'd gone through a six-pack at least, and the minute I walked through the door, he said I didn't know I had a faggot for a son. Faggot. That was one of the nicer things he called me."

"I'm sorry," I murmur. I don't know what else to say.

"Faggot," Luke continues, his words harsh and foreign as they fall from his lips. "Queer, homo, slut. Called me a cunt once, too, can you even *do* that? I mean, that just doesn't make sense, you know? But it doesn't take the sting away."

My heart breaks as the first tear slips down his cheek and he brushes at it roughly. "I know."

"Told me I was lucky my ma was dead." I place a comforting hand on his shoulder and his voice breaks. "Told me she'd kill herself if she was alive and knew I was such a fuck-up. Knew I fucked *guys*. I *hate* him."

He covers his mouth with his hand and squeezes his eyes shut, and suddenly I'm struck at how young he is all over again. Without thinking, I wrap my arms around him and he's in my embrace, where I've wanted him all day, only his tears are hot against my shirt and his shoulders shake as I rub his back and tell him it's okay.

"I had to leave," he mumbles into my neck and I nod, yes, I see that. He had to leave, and he's here now, his dad's not going to hurt him anymore. I tell him this even though it's no consolation, the damage is already done, but Luke nods and lets me hold him, his arms finding their way around my waist to hug me tight.

✽

WHEN THE TEARS ARE dry and he sniffles an apology, I wipe his cheeks with my shirt sleeve and tell him it's okay. "Come on," I say, motioning at the tub overflowing with suds. "The water's getting cold."

That makes him laugh. "I seriously doubt *that*." But he's grinning, that's what I hoped for, and before I can turn away, he unzips his jeans and pushes them down. I look at his feet so I won't stare at his long legs, his lean thighs, the bulge in the front of his underwear, and when those briefs hit the ground, I close my eyes. I hear a faint splash, then Luke draws in a sharp breath as he sinks into the tub. This late in the day, the water from the hose must be pretty hot. When he's settled, Luke says, "You can look now."

I laugh as I open my eyes, a quick comment on the tip of my tongue, but he's in that damn cowboy hat, pushed back so I can see his piercing eyes, his full lips, and above the suds his shoulders are bare and freckled and damp, and all I can do is clear my throat and look away.

Kent will be home soon. Then this silliness will stop, Luke won't be such a temptation with my lover around, Kent will douse this stupid crush real quick.

But is there harm in looking? In watching the way Luke runs a hand up one arm and down the other, trailing water along skin that glistens in the slanting sun? He had to keep that hat on, didn't he? Does he even realize what that *does* to me? I fell for Kent before I even saw his face—just the hat and the jeans and the bare back, and I was gone. *You better watch it,* I tell myself as Luke frowns up at me. The shadow from his brim lies across the smooth skin above his upper lip. *You'll end up falling for this one, too.* "What 'cha thinking?" he wants to know.

How much I want you right this minute, I reply silently. *How I still feel your warmth in my arms, your breath on my neck. How I'm pretty sure I'm not going to close my eyes when you get out of that tub.* But I don't say that. Instead I shrug and mumble, "Nothing really." Nothing he needs to know.

"Hmm." He sinks down and lays his head back, the hat pushing forward over his brow. His knees peek through the suds in front of his chest and his arms stretch out around the aluminum sides of the tub, gripping the warm tin. "This is nice," he says, speaking low. With a shy grin, he winks at me. "Too bad it's only big enough for one."

I can see that now, Kent pulling into the driveway to find me crammed into that tiny tub behind Luke. Somehow I don't think that'll go over too well. Shoving my hands deep into the pockets of my jeans, I tell myself that's not the start of an erection pressing against my fingers. "Do you do this often?" he asks. He trails a hand through the suds, parting them, and I catch a glimpse of his chest beneath the water before the soap drifts back together again. "Just sit out here in the sun? Does your friend do it, too?"

With a laugh, I admit, "Kent rarely *showers.*" I suspect he thinks bathing is beneath him. "He—no. He doesn't use that tub."

Luke looks at me openly, like it doesn't bother him that once those

Cowboy 27

suds dry up, nothing will hide his nakedness from me. "But you do," he says, trailing his hand through the water again.

Don't ask if I jerk off in it, I pray. The last thing he needs to know is that since the showerhead broke I've been out in that tub every morning, rubbing myself beneath the tepid water, whimpering as my fingers dance over my thighs, my balls, and the main reason I use so much soap is to hide my cum when I pour the water out on the ground. I can't help it—if Kent gave me what I needed at night, I wouldn't have to do things myself. As it is I get him once, maybe twice a month, and last night wasn't even worth it. I'm still disgusted about that.

Luke doesn't ask, thank God, just slips down lower into the suds and moans as the water soothes away the day. I can imagine his muscles relaxing, his skin softening, and shouldn't I be doing something else right about now? Making dinner, maybe? Closing up the lot, *something*? Anything other than standing here and staring at him like a sex-crazed pervert. And I *am* staring, it's evident when Luke asks me for a washcloth and I jump at the sound of his voice. A washcloth, right—there's one hanging on a peg inside the barn with the towel I use to dry myself off after a bath. As I approach the tub with it in hand, Luke sits up and leans forward and asks, "Can you maybe wash my back? I don't think I can reach."

His back. Bare and wet. I can see his shoulder blades curved like wings where he's hunched over, and the nubs of his spine stand out like knuckles. I want to run my tongue around them, each and every one, count my way down from his neck to his hips and why stop there? Lick down over his tailbone, between his cheeks, where he's tender. I want to hold his thighs in my hands as I rim him, my tongue doing things that will bring tears to his eyes, he'll *beg* for release, things I've only dreamed of doing because Kent's not into kinky shit like that.

Luke though, I see in his eyes that he'll let me have him any way I want, he'll grip the sheets of my bed as I finger him, he'll cry out my name if I want him to. It's all there in his purple gaze, all the things he'd let me do to him, all the things I hunger to do.

His back. "Marcus?" he asks, concerned. "If you don't want to, it's okay. I understand…"

I shake my sordid thoughts away. "No, I can." Kneeling behind him, I dip the washcloth into the mild water, then run a trepidatious hand up the curve of his back. Through the thin terrycloth, his skin is hot from the sun and water, and this close I can smell the laundry fresh scent of the soap, the lingering sweat that beads along his flesh. But I don't think of that, or the firm muscles beneath my hand as I rub along his back, or the contented way he sighs when my fingers work at the knots in his neck. Over his shoulders, down his arms, down his back and into the water and I'm not thinking about what I'm touching now, what I'm just inches away from, I'm *not*. Up his spine again, around his neck, over his throat, and when he leans back against me, I hardly notice the water that splashes onto my jeans or the warm press of his skin through my shirt. My hand is on his chest now, the other one pushing at my erection, I have to close my eyes as one hand drifts lower down his body and the other works my own hard cock through my jeans. God, if Kent sees this…

He's not here.

My hand trails down over Luke's flat stomach until a thick shaft pokes at me. "Marcus," he murmurs, gripping the edges of the tub, and when I encircle his erection, he hisses my name again.

The washcloth floats away. I take him in hand, he's bigger than I had imagined, huge beneath the water, and as hard as I am. Easing down my zipper, I stroke myself through my boxers as I cup his balls, my fingers entwining in hair like seaweed at his crotch. Slowly, I fondle his dick, rubbing up his length to the spongy tip and then back to the thick base, my hand squeezing and kneading until he gasps my name. He's lying back on my shoulder now, his lips against my ear, and his small moans and thin sighs spur me on, I work at us both, finding a steady rhythm that brings my cock from my boxers and makes him thrust into my hand.

I'm not doing this, I think even as I pick up the pace to bring him release. *This isn't me,* as I press my lips to his cheek, but he's salty and soft and when I kiss him again, his mouth finds mine.

I was right. He's just as sweet, as hot, as ripe as I thought he would be.

✷

WHEN HIS COCK SPASMS in my hand and he moans my name, his hand grasping at my knee, I come in a spurt that drips down the side of the tub and into the grass. I can't even remember the last time I got off with someone, *anyone*, sure as hell not Kent. *Kent*—

The name is like cold water on my erection, and suddenly Luke's body against mine is too hot, scalding almost. I feel dirty and soiled and what the *fuck* am I doing here? Massaging this boy in one hand, playing with myself in the other, right out in the backyard where anyone can see, anyone at all, and my lover's on his way home, this is so damn *wrong* no matter how right it feels. Embarrassed, I pull my hand from the tub, my sleeve wet to my elbow where I reached into the water, and when Luke kisses my jaw, I turn away.

"Jesus," I mutter—what am I *doing* here? This isn't me, I'm not this bad, I'm not one to cheat on someone I love and I love Kent, don't I? Not this boy I just met, I can't throw away two years of my life on a moment of weakness, I won't. I love Kent, I do. I do.

I have to.

Without looking at Luke, I tuck myself back into my boxers, zip up my damp jeans, wipe my hands on my thighs, both of them, they are equally stained. Luke sits up and frowns at me as I stand and run a hand through my short hair. I smell sex and wipe my hand on my jeans again. "Marcus?" he asks, concerned. When he reaches for me, I move away, but I can hear him rise from the tub, water splashing down around him, and he's naked now, I won't turn around, I *can't*. "Marcus, wait."

His hand touches my elbow, his fingers wet and warm and strong through my sleeve. "Wait," he says again. "It's not...I mean, that wasn't—we didn't really *do* anything."

"I'm with Kent," I tell him. Did I forget to mention that somewhere along the way? Did I forget to tell him that I have a lover who thinks I'm here alone now, who trusts that the only pleasure I'll find today comes from my own hand? *You used your hand*, a voice in my head whispers with a hint of malicious glee. I laugh bitterly and comb my fingers through my hair again, just to shake Luke off. He's standing naked behind me, water runneling down the planes of his body, his cock probably still half-erect and pointing at me—reaching for the towel I set on the picnic table earlier, I hold it over my shoulder and close my eyes tight. "Just cover yourself up, will you?"

He takes the towel. "I'm sorry," he mumbles. I hear the rasp of terry-cloth on skin and damn him for being like this, so irresistible, so luscious. Damn *me* for being so weak. "Marcus, really, I didn't...I don't see how it's so bad."

With another short laugh, I shake my head and blink quickly at the setting sun. When is Kent coming back? Is he on the road now, a few miles away? Or still at the bar, lost in his cups? Where is he when I need him here with me? To keep me safe, to keep me from Luke, from *myself*—where *is* he? "Kissing you and feeling you up and getting you off," I say, hating the way my voice almost breaks because despite all that, it wasn't enough, was it? I still want more. "Try telling Kent how it's not so bad. I'd like to see how you explain it to *him*."

"He doesn't have to know." An unsure hand touches my back, and then Luke asks softly, "When's the last time he kissed you, Marcus? He didn't last night."

I have to agree, no, not last night. I press my lips together into a thin line and tell myself it's not tears that sting my eyes, it's the sunlight and the heat and the bugs because I don't cry. Cowboys don't cry. *Luke did*—but I'm not thinking of that, or the way he felt in my embrace or in my hand, or the way he tastes, I'm *not*. "You're amazing," he's saying, and though I tell myself that I'm not paying attention, I hang on his every word. "Does he ever tell you that? Don't you think you deserve something more that a drunk fuck? When's the last time he kissed you, or hugged you for no reason, or looked at you the way you've been looking at me all day? This morning, maybe, before he left? Did he kiss you then?"

Numb, I shake my head. "I didn't see him," I admit. "We don't—" With a sigh, I cover my face with one hand and still smell the lingering musk of cum in my palm. "We have separate rooms, Luke. He doesn't want to wake me when he gets up so early."

"And he doesn't want to hold you while he sleeps." The disgust in Luke's voice makes me rub at my eyes until red flowers bloom in my darkness. His hands are so damn gentle when he touches my shoulders, rubs at my arms. I can smell the warm water that clings to him, he's so close behind me, and I can almost feel his body along mine. *Wishful thinking.* "You need to be kissed," he whispers into the back of my neck, and to prove his point, he kisses my skin, a tender press of his lips that makes my own tremble. He kneads my shoulders in a slow massage. "You need to be loved, Marcus. You can't do it yourself and *he's* not doing it—"

"So what, you're applying for the job?" My voice is harsh to my own ears, but when Luke nuzzles into my hair and sighs my name, I choke as I ask, "What's it to you anyway?"

I don't really expect a reply. He's just passing through, looking for a quick fuck and he happened to get lucky enough to stumble onto someone looking for more, someone like me. But he kisses my neck, my jaw, and then he says, "No one's ever told me I had pretty eyes before." I laugh—God, did I say that? This morning, at the sink, I should've never said that. "Of all the boys I've known," Luke continues in that same low voice, "you're the only one who looks at me like you'd give up everything for me. That's a hard look to deny."

Like you'd give up everything... and that's exactly what I have to lose.

❋

LUKE IS RIGHT, WE don't have to tell Kent. He doesn't have to know about the whole tub thing, best not to mention it. Ideally maybe even Luke will be gone before he comes home, but to be honest I don't *want* him to leave. So I pick his clothes up from the grass as he wraps the towel around his waist, and I tell him that I'll see what I have in my closet that will fit him while these run through the wash. No use putting dirty clothes on a clean body, is there? He trails behind me into the house, quiet because I've sort of brushed aside what he said—I don't want to talk about what I need, I don't want to think about Kent right now, and I sure as hell don't want to talk about jerking Luke off in the tub because he might hear how eager I am for more of his kisses, his touch, and God only knows what *that* will lead.

I try to tell myself I don't want to find out.

Inside, Luke follows me down the hall to the bedrooms, stopping when I do at the laundry closet to shove his jeans and shirt into the washer. They're the only clothing in the washer but I run a load anyway, the sooner he's fully dressed, the better. As it is I can't look at him directly, there's too much skin, too much *nakedness,* his arms bunched in thin muscles and crossed in front of his chest, his stomach firm and sculpted like clay, a thin line of hair leading from his navel down that flat muscle to the towel that rides low on his hips and further, to a thick patch that I know twines easily in my fingers and a hard shaft that even now pokes at the terrycloth with a slight lump.

And below the towel, his legs, so strong, so lean, covered in a fuzzy down of drying hair that captures the light like an aura surrounding him. I want to smooth that hair beneath my hands, pet it flat like a cat's coat, until it's straight and long and I'll lick it down if I have to, just to make it stay. I want to lick him, his legs, his stomach, his arms, his neck and chest and cock, and he can see the desire in my eyes, he said he could and that's why he wants me so bad—how am I supposed to hide that from Kent? How will he not see it too?

Almost rudely, I step around Luke to enter my bedroom, hating the way my body thrills when my hand brushes his hip in passing. My room is sparsely furnished, like the rest of the house—a cowboy's room, definitely, with the narrow bed and small table beside it, a lamp and a clock on top of that, a small dresser, a closet, one huge potted Jamaican agave in the corner that is the only gift Kent's ever given me. As I pull open a drawer on my dresser and start to rummage through my jeans, Luke sits on the edge of my bed and looks around. I see him from the corner of my eye. "What size are you?" I ask.

"You should know that," he replies with a coy grin. Toying with the flap of the towel that rests across his thigh, he asks, "Or do you want to feel it again? What's this?"

Before I can answer, he bends down and picks up my folder of magazine ads, half-hidden beneath the bed. "Nothing," I tell him, but he's already flipping through the pictures of my boys inside. I should photograph him, sitting on my bed like he is, cross-legged, bare-chested, that damn hat cocked so far back on his head that I'm surprised it's still on. "It's nothing, Luke, put it down. What size pants do you wear? I'm thirty-four, thirty-six." He doesn't answer, doesn't look up from the ads that Ally so carefully tore out from her magazines and sent to me. "Luke—"

"You have a thing for cowboys, don't you?" he asks, closing the folder. When I open my mouth to speak, he adds, "Thirty-two but if you have a belt, that'll work. Who sends you these?"

"My sister." I pull out a pair of faded jeans, worn but clean, and grab a braided belt from the back of the closet door. Then I find a t-shirt he can wear, a long-sleeved shirt, a pair of boxers that he'll have to roll to keep up, and I lay the clothes out on the bed. "I'll let you get dressed—" I start, reaching for the folder.

He hands it over. "Pretty boys," he says, standing, and as I head for the door, he tells me, "You don't have to leave."

"I think it's better I do," I tell him. I don't need to see him naked by my bed, that image would sear itself into my mind and haunt me on lonely nights, I don't need that. "I'll just get dinner started..."

The towel around his waist falls to the floor. His skin is golden in the light from my lamp, and he looks over the clothes as if his nakedness doesn't bother him. "You think these'll fit?" he asks, holding up my boxers, *mine,* but I can't tear my gaze from the dark V of his crotch, the length that hangs between his legs, the firm buttocks that clench when he bends to step into the underwear. "You don't mind if I wear these, do you?" he asks. When I can't answer, he looks up at me, concerned. "Marcus?"

Then the boxers are up, they hide his genitals and ass and my heart starts to beat again, I can breathe, I can think, he's talking to me. "Marcus?" he's saying, and I nod because I'm listening, even if I can't stop staring. "You don't mind?"

"No," I manage. *Dinner,* my mind whispers, and I have this vision of the two of us in the kitchen, our chairs pulled close together, candles flickering in the middle of the table and me feeding him from my plate. I see his purple eyes flash in the candlelight—I see him lying me back across the table and unbuttoning my shirt, unzipping my jeans, stroking at me through my boxers, kissing and sucking and rubbing until I scream with want of him, and when he finally enters me, I grasp at the sides of the table, Kent's never felt this good, this wicked, this *right* in me, *ever*—

Luke interrupts the daydream. "You said something about dinner?" he

Cowboy

asks, and he's almost fully dressed now, my t-shirt pulled up to expose his stomach as he cinches my jeans with my belt.

I'll wear those before I wash them again, and I'll stand right where he's standing now, I'll pull the zipper down and fondle myself through the boxers he wears, I'll come just thinking about him in my clothes and that folder beneath my bed won't have to be open then. I'll smear those jeans and boxers with my juices and remember his dick in my hand, I'll pretend it's him I'm getting off, I'll whisper his name when I come. After he leaves, of course, when all I have is Kent and he's nothing to get worked up over anymore, is he? Not when I have Luke in my memory.

"Dinner," I echo, nodding. Yes, dinner, sounds good.

I wonder if we have any candles.

✸

WE EAT CHILI BECAUSE we're low on groceries and that's one of the reasons Kent went into town in the first place, to restock our pantry. But there's enough ground beef left, and I find a can of beans in the cabinets— cut up some tomatoes from the garden, add a blend of spices that Kent keeps in a bag marked *hot!* above the fridge, serve with bread and butter. Luke sits at the head of the table, Kent's chair, where he sat this morning for breakfast, and as we eat I find out more about him than I know about my lover of two years. He loves strawberries, his first name's Samuel, he graduated fifth in his class at the high school and surprised everyone by not even bothering to apply to college.

"I just needed to get out of there," he tells me, dipping bread into the chili until it's red with sauce, then tearing into it as I watch him eat, wishing he would bite into me like that. He might if I ask, he seems the easy-going type. I can't ask. I shouldn't even be *thinking* stuff like this, not while he's just talking to me and Kent's on his way home. "What with my dad and all," Luke says with a shrug.

I nod like I know what he means and memorize the way his Adam's apple bobs when he swallows.

He tells me about a dog he had when he was a little boy, a black lab named Baron that followed him around everywhere, even though he dwarfed Luke. He tells me that he keeps a picture of his momma in a wallet, which he hid in our barn last night after he ate the burger. "Just to keep it safe," he says. I don't ask where it is and he doesn't offer the information.

He asks about my sister, Ally, who left New Jersey when I did but kept going west—wound up in LA, out by the coast, says I should come out and pay her a visit but there aren't any cowboys there to interest me. He asks about my folks, both doctors at the hospital where I was born, both retired and living somewhere down in the Florida Keys now, last I heard. I don't keep up with them much, a card at Christmas, that's about it. He asks about the scar on the back of my hand, where I cut myself opening a can of tuna last week and it hasn't quite healed yet. He asks me things Kent doesn't even care to know, and by the time we're finished eating, I know him better than I do myself.

"I like you," he says, in the same tone of voice he used when he told me he likes going to baseball games and eating hot dogs slathered with mustard and ketchup and onions. "I want to kiss you again," so nonchalant, like he's talking about something he plans to do tomorrow, bring in the crops or water the lawn or take the tractor to town to get it fixed.

He leans back in his seat, one elbow draped over the back, one arm on the table just inches from mine. Reaching out, he tucks a piece of hair behind my ear, his fingers tender on my face. Outside I hear a car on the road and I sit up enough to see out the window, sure it's Kent, he's home, he'll ruin this—

But the car continues on, not stopping, not even slowing down, its headlights dwindling away into the distance. As I sink back to my seat, unnerved, Luke brushes at my cheek again, smoothing his thumb over the faint hair that's begun to grow in above my upper lip. "Can I?" he asks.

I pretend that I'm not sure what he wants. "What?" I should clean up now, put the plates in the sink and check on the wash, anything but sit here and let him touch me like this, let him talk to me so softly.

With a gentle hand, he cups my chin, turns me towards him, and suddenly he's right *there*, his face inches from mine. "Can I kiss you again?" he wants to know. I stare into his violet eyes and my throat works around words that I can't manage to say. *No*, I should tell him, but that's not what my heart wants, he sees that in my face and before I can reply, he closes his eyes and leans close, closer, his lips already parted, his tongue licking out of his mouth and into mine.

I grip his wrist but instead of pushing him away, I pull him closer.

He stumbles from his chair into my lap, his mouth insistent, his tongue probing into me, tasting me, filling me and my arms find his waist, pull him down into my lap, curve over his ass as our kiss deepens. His hands are on me now, roaming through my hair, down my neck, his breath hot, his lips demanding, and the next time a car passes outside I don't bother to see if it's Kent.

I don't care right now—all I want is Luke's welcome weight on my

Cowboy 35

thighs, his knee pressing into my groin, his arms holding me so tightly, his lips on mine.

※

SOMETIME LATER THE PHONE rings, startling us. We're both breathless and flushed, Luke's shirt on the floor and mine unbuttoned, pushed aside. My nipples ache from the wonderful things he does with his tongue, swirling around the hardened nubs until I moan from his ministrations, and a dark red welt shines wetly on his shoulder where I sucked at him, the beginnings of a hickey that he's going to have to hide from Kent. *Kent*—the phone rings again and I push Luke away just as he starts to pick at my zipper. "The phone," I say, like he might not hear it. He kisses me again before sliding off my lap.

I have to straighten my jeans when I stand, the denim bites into my crotch and I have to shake it loose, I'm so damn hard and just from *kisses*. I can't imagine how incredible it'd feel to have those lips, that mouth, on other parts of me. Outside past the kitchen window the sun has set, draping the land and the road and our little produce lot in a darkness punctuated only by a rising moon that covers everything in a silver glow. What time is it? Kent should be home by now.

The phone rings a third time and I snatch it up. "Hello?" I ask. It'll be him, calling from the bar to tell me he's running late. *No shit.*

But it's not him, it's a woman's voice that fills my ear. "Mr. Latham?" she asks, and I know something's wrong because no one misters me. "I'm Officer Schultz, with the county police? There's been an accident—"

"Oh God." The floor falls out from under me, *an accident,* and Luke is there to catch me, he wraps his arms around me, holds me as I start to shake. *An accident.* While I'm here kissing on another boy, my lover is… "Kent?" I ask, my voice quivering. Luke eases me to the floor, sits so close that he's almost on top of me, smoothes my hair and my brow and murmurs it's okay. It's *not* okay. "Kent," I say again. I can't remember what he looks like now, and my heart hurts with each beat. "Is he okay? My God, what kind of accident? Tell me he's okay."

"He's fine."

The officer's voice is dry and humorless but I feel like she's just saying that because I asked her to. She starts to read from a police report—driving too fast, she calls him *Mr. Smithson* and at first I don't realize she means Kent, no one calls him that, until she says he took a curve at break-neck speed and a showerhead on the seat beside him rolled to the floor. He reached down to get it out from under his feet, that's something he would do while driving, veered over the line and almost hit an oncoming car, a policeman of all people. Looked up in time to see the lights and pulled hard to the right, off the road and into a ditch. "He's fine," Officer Schultz assures me again, am I crying here? I don't know. "But he's pretty shaken up and has a blood alcohol level of almost twice the legal limit." She stops, waiting for my response.

"He's okay," I whisper, and Luke rests his head against my back, his arms tightening around my waist. "Where is he? Can I talk to him?"

"We had to book him," she says, sounding like one of those cops on TV, *book him*. "He passed out the minute we got him in a cell." *A cell, Jesus.* Arrested. I wonder how many drinks he had before he thought he could try to make it home. My fear is slowly turning to anger, what the *fuck* was he thinking? That he'd sober up on the drive back? That he wouldn't be stopped? He has a lead foot, I've told him before it'll get him in trouble.

"He's posted bail," she continues, and I wonder how much of our deposit is left after *that*. "But we're going to keep him here until morning. He wanted me to give you a call so you wouldn't worry. I won't kid you, he's going to have to appear in court, and there's a good chance he'll lose his license for awhile, but other than that, he'll be fine."

Fine. "Okay," I mumble. I let the phone slip from my fingers, I'm too dazed to hang it back up. *Fine.*

Luke takes the phone, thanks the officer, stands to hang up the receiver. Then his strong hands slip beneath my arms, help me to my feet. "It's okay," he tells me, brushing my hair up off my brow, but I feel my lips tug into an ugly pout and I'm just not so sure anymore. He could've been killed—*but he wasn't,* I remind myself. He *could've* though, that's the thing, and I'm here with Luke and I shouldn't be doing what we were doing, I shouldn't be thinking what I'm thinking, he could've *died*... "Marcus?" Luke asks, rubbing my back. It's such a comforting gesture, I can't help but lean into it. His arms come up around my shoulders and he kisses my cheek tenderly. "He wasn't hurt, right? So it's okay, he's okay."

"It's my fault," I murmur. I wasn't even thinking about him, I was too busy getting lost in Luke, and look what happened, I almost lost him. *My fault...* "I should've gone with him today," I say, nodding when Luke shakes his head. "I could've been driving, this wouldn't have happened, it's my fault really—"

Luke's eyes flash with something I can't read, anger? Conviction? "You're not the one who makes him drink," he tells me. "No matter what he says, you hear me? You have no control over that."

Cowboy 37

I shake his hands off me, what am I doing? My lover sleeps in a holding cell tonight and I'm all over this other boy. *Luke,* I think, even as I extract myself from his embrace. "Maybe you should just sleep on the couch," I say, though we hadn't discussed it and I wasn't seriously going to offer him *my* bed, was I? I don't know. My voice is distant to my ears when I tell him, "I have some extra blankets—"

"Sure," Luke agrees. He touches my shoulder tentatively. When I don't pull away he rubs down my arm, comforting. "The couch is fine, Marcus, really." With a smile, he winks and adds, "Better than the barn."

When I give him a wan grin, he sighs. "He'll be home tomorrow, he's fine." I nod, yes, tomorrow, but then what? What happens to this sudden intimacy that's sprung up between Luke and myself when Kent is back? What happens to the kisses and the touches and my own adulterous thoughts? What then?

The couch. I think if we hadn't been interrupted, I might have taken his kisses and his hands into my bedroom, given myself to him and it's a damn good thing that phone rang, it is, because if he spent the night with me, what would Kent do when he came home to that? "Jesus," I mutter. What the fuck have I gotten myself into?

※

BLANKETS FROM THE HALL closet, a pillow off the bed—I have several, I can spare one, and when Luke leaves, I'll bury my face in it and breathe deep the scent of his hair, and this isn't helping here, is it? I shouldn't think shit like this.

"Here you go," I say, dumping the blankets and pillow onto the couch.

He sits in Kent's recliner in just his boxers, his pants on the floor with his shirt, *my* shirt. He leans forward and watches me, and just to keep from looking back, I busy myself with spreading the blankets out along the cushions. I lay bed sheets down over the couch, then a thin comforter, folded up at one end so he can crawl under it easily enough, and I fluff the pillow as I set it at the other end. "There."

The open blanket looks inviting. If he lies down before I turn in, it's going to take all the strength I have not to join him, so I turn away as he stands. "You should be comfortable enough—"

He catches my wrist. When I look at him, I see in his eyes that he wants me in that makeshift bed with him, he wants my arms around him in sleep, he wants to hold me and kiss me and I shouldn't but I can't help it, I can't stop myself as I lean close and press my lips to his. A brief kiss, nothing much, no tongue, no open lips, but it's so gentle, so tender, that I have to squeeze my eyes shut against sudden tears. Tomorrow Kent comes back and this is gone.

"Night," Luke breathes.

"Night," I whisper. I stare into his face for a long moment, searing his image into my memory—the exact shade of his eyes, the deep color of pansies; the shape of his eyelashes, his brows; the length of his nose and his wide mouth, his full lips; the milk-laced coffee color of his skin. I'll dream of him tonight, I already know it. I'll lie in my bed the way I do every night, alone, and it won't be Kent I ache for but this boy, Luke, asleep just a few feet away.

Tomorrow this all ends.

part 2

I'm at the stove scrambling eggs for Luke when Kent comes home. I hear tires on the gravel and crane my neck to look out the kitchen window just as the truck pulls to a stop in front of the porch. *Kent.* I can can see him through the windshield, that black cowboy hat pulled down low over his eyes, a scowl already in place on his lips. When he gets out of the truck and slams the door shut behind him, I forget how to breathe.

From here he's everything I want him to be, shirtless and tan, his face closed, his jeans tight across his ass. I can't believe I thought of cheating on him, I can't believe I let myself get carried away yesterday—what the hell was I thinking? The women who visit our produce stand would *kill* for what I have, that man out in the yard, Kent, and I was all too ready to just throw him away. Luke asked if I love him and standing here by the stove, watching him lean into the back of the pickup for the groceries he bought in town, right this instant? I love him completely.

"He's home," I whisper, turning off the stove. When I glance at Luke, sitting at the table, I see those eyes like purple fire staring back and I almost hear my heart tear in two, it's an audible pain that clenches my chest and makes me wince because I love him, too. I do, I knew it last night, I fell for him between the handjob and his kisses, and I want him as badly as I want Kent when he's sober. My heart twists in half, one part held almost negligently in my lover's hands, the other fisted tight in this boy's palms. I don't want either of them to let go.

I hear heavy boots on the porch and Luke turns away, releasing me from the prison of his gaze. I hurry out the screen door and meet Kent just as he's reaching for the knob. "Hey," I sigh. This close the stench of alcohol makes me dizzy, so strong so early in the morning, and I have to lean back against the door to get some fresh air. I notice a cut on his forehead, half-hidden by the brim of his hat, and another one along his cheek, blood still beaded on his skin. Tentatively, I reach out to touch the scratch but he brushes my hand away. "Are you okay?" I ask, my fingers trembling as I curl them into a useless fist. "Jesus, you scared the hell out of me, do you know that? I didn't know what to think—"

"I'm fine," he mutters. Then he shoves the grocery bags into my arms and I stagger beneath their sudden weight. "You gonna give me some help here?" Before I can respond, he adds, "I don't want to talk about it."

"Okay." He means the arrest. Fine, I can understand that—a night in jail, I don't think I'd want to talk about it, either. I juggle the bags as he heads back to the truck, and one slips from my arms as Luke opens the screen door to catch it. "Thanks," I say, keeping my voice low. He takes the other bag as well, then gives me a tight smile before he disappears into the house. I turn to find Kent standing at the side of the truck, two more bags in hand, staring at me.

At Luke.

Shit.

Despite the fact that I'm barefoot, I trot down the porch steps and hurry to him, careful to step mostly on the grass so I don't cut my feet on the stones. As I try to take the bags from him, he holds the handles tight. "Who the hell is that?" he wants to know.

A million answers flit through my head and disappear, leaving only the truth behind. "Luke," I tell him, like that should mean something.

"Luke," he echoes. Suddenly he lets go of the bags and I stumble away from him. Behind me the screen door slams. I don't have to look to know that Luke is on the porch watching us. "Who the *fuck* is Luke?"

"Kent," I start. I see the anger in his eyes and set the groceries on the ground. When I reach for him, he shrugs me off, he *always* does that. "Look, it's not what you think—"

"What is it then?" he asks. He looks from me to the porch and back again, his face hard lines, his mouth drawn down in a bitter scowl. I try to touch his arm but he slaps my hand away. "I'm gone for one night and come home to *this*?"

I cover my eyes with one hand and sigh. "It's not..." *What you think,* I want to tell him, but that's a lie, isn't it? What exactly *is* he thinking, anyway? I'd give anything right this moment to find that out. "It's not that, Kent, trust me." I speak softly so my words won't carry to the porch, I don't want Luke to overhear me. "He's just a runaway, look at him. He's barely even twenty. I found him sleeping in the barn yesterday—"

"And you didn't call the cops?" Kent asks, but the edge in his voice is gone, and when I touch his arm again, he turns to get the other bags from the back of the truck. At least he doesn't push me away—he lets me step closer, lean against him, press my face against the sweaty flat of his back, and I take shallow breaths so I don't have to smell him, I'm already woozy just being this close.

"You didn't turn his ass out?" he asks.

I shake my head against the spot between his shoulder blades, wrap my arms around his waist. At least he's letting me touch him. Thank God for that.

"He's not a dog, Marcus," he tells me, his arms flexing on either side of me as he hefts the bags from the back of the truck to set them on the ground at our feet. "You can't just keep him like a pet."

"I know," I murmur. "I was just being nice, Kent, that's all. I thought maybe give him a warm meal, a soft bed—"

"Yours?" he asks with a derisive snort. "Or mine?"

"The couch, babe," I say, rubbing his stomach. "He slept on the couch last night."

Kent turns in my embrace, drapes one arm around my shoulders, glares at Luke on the porch and I don't look up at the boy, I can't meet his gaze. "How long is he gonna stay?" Kent asks.

I shrug. "Few days," I say, unsure myself. *Forever,* my heart cries out, the half that Luke holds in his hands, but Kent's here now and whatever Luke and I did yesterday won't happen again. "He helped out with the market," I tell him, as if to prove the boy's worth. After Kent's remark, I feel like a child begging to keep a stray animal and I look up at him, trying to see beneath that hat to his enigmatic eyes. "Maybe just until he heads on, okay?"

Kent stares across the yard and now I look up to see Luke standing there on our porch like it's his home and we're trespassing on his property—with his hands on his hips, my clothes on his thin frame, his purple eyes dark with shadows. He smells clean, I know because he hugged me first thing this morning, woke up and padded into the kitchen with just his boxers on, *my* boxers, and I was already at the stove cooking breakfast. He just wrapped his arms around my waist, kissed the back of my neck, hugged me close and whispered that he had the most wonderful dreams last night. "About you," he said, and when I looked at him, the next kiss landed on my lips. And that was just overnight—Kent's been gone a full day and he hasn't kissed me yet. I love kisses, not drunken ones, sloppy and acidic, but Luke's kisses, heady and rich and sweet, I love those.

Pulling away from me, Kent shakes himself free and says, "It's getting hot, Marcus. Don't hang all over me, I'm right here."

Almost grateful, I step back. That's the difference between these men, isn't it? Kent doesn't want to be touched and Luke can't keep his hands to himself. Me, I'm caught in the middle, because despite the way I feel for one, I can't help but want the other.

✻

THE SILENCE IN THE kitchen between the three of us is deadly. Luke sits at the table—in my seat now, not Kent's, he plopped down there and the look my lover gave him was enough to make him switch chairs without a word—and he shovels in his eggs, watching me as he eats like he's waiting for my lead. Kent puts the groceries away, storming around the kitchen with stiff steps, throwing cans into the cabinets and slamming doors shut, the look on his face curbing anything I might want to say.

There's nothing *to* say, really—the easy talk between Luke and me is gone, replaced with an unnerving tension that hangs over us like a funeral pall. Every time Kent brushes by me, I jump. I want to ask about the showerhead but don't, I feel his mood building like thunderclouds, I don't want his anger to rain down on me today.

So I busy myself with the dishes, and I make a pot of coffee because I know he likes his java in the morning. When it perks, I pour him a mug and set it on the table to cool. Luke stares at me as I lean past him but I avoid his gaze. I can't look at him, not here. If I do, Kent will see the desire in my eyes, the openness in Luke's, and he'll know what happened yesterday, the tub, the kisses, he'll see it all in that one look.

So I avoid Luke's violet eyes and when I turn to the sink, I feel his hot gaze sear my back. *What now?* I want to know. What the hell happens now?

Kent doesn't ask Luke where he's from or where he's headed. I don't expect him to. Still, when I can't take the quiet any longer, I offer up the information. "He's from where did you say? Near San Angelo?" I glance over my shoulder at Luke, who has finished his eggs and picks through the strawberries now. I remember the one he dipped in sugar yesterday and fed to me. When he meets my gaze, he rims his lips with a piece of tender fruit and I know he's thinking the same thing. He tastes sweet like those berries—I'd give anything to taste him again. Shaking the thought away, I ask, "Isn't that what you told me? San Angelo?"

With a shrug, Luke takes a quick look at Kent's back—he's reaching into the cabinets above the refrigerator, ignoring us both—and then winks at me. A thrill runs through me at that secret gesture. "Somewhere near there," he murmurs. His lips are red from the berries, and I love the way his throat works when he swallows the fruit down.

He takes another strawberry, runs it around the sugar bowl until it's coated white, then eases it into his mouth, sucking at the fruit greedily, his eyes never leaving mine. *This could be you,* those eyes say, and I have to clench my hands in the dishtowel to keep from going to him, I *want* it to be me. His cheeks suck in, his lips work around the fruit, his tongue licks off the sugar and he's still watching me, I can't look away. *I could do this to you.* I see the promise in his face, his lips, his hands. *I know you want me to, suck you like this strawberry until you come in a rush that I'll lick away like sugar. I know you want it from me.*

I do. Oh sweet Jesus in heaven, I do.

But there's Kent, who reaches in front Luke for a strawberry to pop in his mouth, and the seductive spell is broken. "You're a good ways from home, kid," he says, chomping on the fruit. I watch his cheeks—he chews twice, maybe three times, before swallowing. His throat doesn't work in that same mystical way Luke's does, and any sugar that clings to his lips he just brushes away with the back of his hand, he doesn't lick it down. Taking another piece of fruit, Kent wants to know, "So when are you leaving?"

"Kent," I sigh—that's rude.

He gives me an unreadable look and shrugs. "Did you water?" he wants to know.

"I just got up," I tell him. He knows I don't wake up at the crack of dawn like he is—he knows I don't water those plants. Still, I dry my hand on a clean towel and begin, "If you want me to…"

"Never mind." He kicks at one of the grocery bags and I hear the rattle of bottles inside. Beer. "Put the rest of this away," he says and I nod quickly, yes, I can do that. To Luke, he says, "I'm not taking on any freeloaders, kid. You want to eat my food, sleep on my couch, you best earn your keep. I've got vegetables out back ready to come in."

"I can do that," Luke agrees. Kent nods like it's settled, as if letting Luke stay was *his* idea, and I don't say anything. Let him think that, if it makes this easier. Let him believe that Luke's staying here just because Kent asked him to. *It's me,* I want to say but don't, I keep my mouth shut and don't say a word while Kent starts going over the plants he thinks are ready for picking. The peppers, another batch of strawberries, the onions and I know he's giving that to Luke just because he hates digging those bastards out himself. When he's finished, Luke nods, gives me another long look before he pushes away from the table and stretches. My pants fall down his hips slightly, exposing a flash of smooth stomach where my shirt pulls up. I ache to touch him, kiss him again, run my fingers across his belly and beneath his shirt, *my* shirt.

And I can't.

When Kent heads outside to start watering, Luke brings his dishes over to the sink. I don't move away from the counter and his hip bumps mine playfully. "He's all heart," he jokes. Then, noticing my faint smile, he leans on the sink and frowns up at me. "You love *him*?"

I can't reply. Do I? That stoic man out there who didn't kiss me good morning, didn't say he missed me last night, didn't say he was sorry he scared the living hell out of me with that damn accident? This breathless fear that keeps me quiet, is that love? This hunger for a smile, a touch, a kiss, is that? "You know," Luke murmurs, sidling closer until his hip presses against mine, "if you were *my* boy, and that crap happened last night? I'd come home crying for you to forgive me, baby. I'd be so shook up, almost died? The first thing I'd do coming in that door would've been to lay you down and tell you I'd never, ever do that shit again."

If you were MY boy…but I'm not, I think, and as if he hears that thought, Luke looks at his hands, folded and dangling in the sink above his dishes. "But if that was me?" he whispers. "It wouldn't have happened. I don't drink, and I can't imagine I'd ever want to sleep anywhere but with you." With a soft sigh, he adds, "If you were mine."

Through the kitchen window I watch Kent unravel the garden hose and hear those words again. *If you were mine.*

✻

LUKE DISAPPEARS IN THE fields behind the house, one of the paper grocery bags in hand to gather the ripened vegetables. I finish putting away the rest of the things Kent bought in town—the grocery store wasn't the only place he stopped, and I pretend I don't notice the bottles of Jim Beam and Mad Dog and Cuervo even as I put beneath the sink, I ignore the labels on the beer cans as I stow them on the lowest shelf of the fridge. I find the showerhead, hidden beneath rice and beef in one bag, and I consider putting it in myself but think better of it. Kent bought it, he'll want to play the man and install the thing, that's just the way he is. So I leave it on the kitchen table, fold the bags up and stash them in one of the cabinets, then straighten Luke's sheets on the couch.

With no one to see me, I hug the pillow to my face, breathe deep the clean boyish scent that lingers, pick at the few hairs scattered across the surface. I'm alone in the house—Kent out front and Luke out back, no one around, no one to see when I unzip my jeans and slip them down to my ankles, my boxers right behind them. I feel wicked and dirty when I slip between the covers on the couch, but the sheets are warm and soft on my naked skin and I tell myself it's Luke's body heat I'm wrapped up in now.

Rolling onto my stomach, I bury my nose in the pillow and smell him again as my hand trails down to stroke at the hardness between my legs. I rise up on my knees, my ass in the air, my face still pressed in the pillow, the heady scent stronger than any alcohol on Kent's breath. My fingers knead my erection, squeeze my own balls, thumb along the flesh beneath them and I gasp into the pillow, stroke harder, pull at myself, thrust into my hand. The heavy blanket holding me down, that's Luke above me; the soft pillow is his body, I'm breathing him in with each gasp and I sigh his name when I come, a fast spurt that's been aching for release ever since he kissed me this morning.

It's over in a few minutes—wiping my hand on the sheets, I yank my pants back up before anyone can come in and find me here, getting off where the boy slept. With angry hands I strip the sheets from the couch, tear off the pillowcase, ball everything up into embarrassed fists and storm down the hall to the washer. His clothes are still in there, waiting to be dried—I shove the sheets on top of them and run another load.

Then, while I'm thinking of it, I slip into Kent's darkened bedroom, strip his bed down too, holding my breath so I won't catch a whiff of the stale sweat and beer that rises from his sheets like a swampy miasma. Jesus *Christ* but he needs to bathe. Once I have his sheets in the washer, I open the windows in his room just to air the place out. I'm glad I *don't* sleep with him—I'd suffocate in the night.

I put new sheets on his bed, and then on the couch, because seeing the empty cushions reminds me of what I just did. *Guilty pleasures,* I think as I make Luke's "bed." What would've happened if he came in while I was in his sheets jerking off—would he have laughed? Dropped his pants and tore the sheet away to stick it to me? Would it turn him on to know I got off on the faded scent of his hair on my pillow?

He doesn't have to know, I think. Knowing would give him the impression that I want him, and no matter how badly I do, there's Kent to think about,

Cowboy 47

I can't just throw what I have with him away. Two years, an eternity in this Texas heat, and sure he drinks but he's not mean to me, he doesn't hit or yell. Doesn't touch me as much as I'd like and never kisses me really, but I can live with that, can't I?

Can I?

Shaking the doubt away, I head into the kitchen to finish the dishes and see Kent's coffee on the table, the java cool and gummy now like oil in the mug. I dump it in the sink and pour him another cup. He's good to me, Kent is, giving me somewhere to stay, a room of my own and a job in his produce lot, trusting me to run the place when he's in town, loving me…he *does* love me, I know it, regardless of whatever Luke thinks. He hasn't seen how good we are together when Kent's sober. He's never seen the rare smile or felt those rough hands, so beguiling, so tender when they touch me.

When being the operative word—for all the bitching I do, he *is* kind, even if he doesn't touch me enough, doesn't *love* me enough. *He works hard all day,* I tell myself, his cup in hand as I step out on the porch. *He's worn out by the evening, you know that, Marcus. You can't expect him to want to get it up after working out in the hot sun for ten, twelve hours at a time.*

Maybe not, but would it be so bad if he could at least just *cuddle*? Hold me for a little while, instead of heading into his room alone to pass out on his bed? Hell, even just let me hold him, that's all I'm asking for here. *Some sort of affection, you know?*

Like Luke.

Luke looks at me and I feel his gaze like a hand on my body. Why can't Kent look at me like that? Why can't he be as open as Luke was when he said liked my kisses, he wanted to taste me again? Or this morning, *if you were mine…*

I shake my head to clear the words away, I don't need to remember them.

Down by the road, Kent's standing like a lawn ornament, hose in hand as he waters his plants, and the first customers have already pulled over to check out the goods. To check out *him*, that's the reason they're here, blue-haired old ladies who giggle over his tanned skin and whisper to each other that he's like a shot of whiskey, hits you hard at first and burns all the way down. I don't want to think of where that fire he sets in them burns, *God.* Same flames that lick my groin when I look at Luke, I'm sure.

Coming up behind Kent, I hold out the mug and say softly, "Your coffee, babe." When he takes it without looking at me, I sigh and trail a hand down his back. "Thanks for…" *For letting him stay,* I almost said, but then he'll want to know why. So I shrug and settle for just, "Thanks."

Kent sips at his coffee and doesn't reply. I don't expect him to, he's the type of guy who won't answer if he decides he doesn't want to talk about… whatever it is you want to talk about. He'll just ignore you until you feel foolish enough to wander away, that's how he is. I'm used to it by now, don't bother to get all worked up about it anymore. If I'm talking and he doesn't look interested or doesn't respond, I just stop, mid-sentence if I have to, what's the use? A waste of breath, that's all it is. He's not a man of many words.

Unlike Luke, who *likes* to talk. All yesterday, I love the sound of his voice. *And you need to stop comparing them,* I think. *It's not going to work that way. Kent is your lover. Luke is just passing through, keep that in mind.*

I was just passing through myself, two years back.

When Kent doesn't speak, I retreat to the tent and the table by the register and click on my fan. It's hot out here already. Propping my feet up on the table, I lean back in my chair and watch Kent through hooded eyes. He looks amazing from here, black hat, broad back, tanned skin. He glances at me as he waters and I feel a thrill course through me at that look, smoldering, possessive.

At least, from *here* that's what it looks like, but his eyes are shielded, shadowed from the brim of his hat, and I don't know what he's thinking, I can't read his gaze. I tell myself it's about me, that's a comforting thought, but it's probably not. More than likely his mind's on the whiskey flask I see in his back pocket, or his plants, or the customers milling about. He glances at me again later, when he starts to pour the contents of that flask into his coffee, and I look away. He tells himself I don't see and me? I let him believe that.

By noon things are almost back to normal—he's dumped at least half of that flask into his mug and the tension is gone from his shoulders, the anger I sensed roiling in him when he came home this morning has evaporated like water in the heat of the day. Already yesterday seems like a half-remembered dream, me sitting in this same spot with an uncanny feeling of *déjà vu* as I watched Luke where Kent is now, and when *he* looked at me, it *was* with a hungry look, and a slight smile to add to my fantasies. But he's not here today, just me and Kent and I can almost believe he never existed, just a dream torn from between the covers of my sister's magazines.

His kisses, though, those were real, I still taste them. At the register I rub my lips with an ice cube from my glass of water and imagine my fingers are his, rimming my mouth with the ice before he leans down to kiss me, his tongue plunging into me, demanding, his hands on my chest like they were last night, smoothing down my stomach to the ache in my jeans—

Someone leans down behind me, startling me from the daydream. As I struggle to sit up, my jeans bite into my erection, I pick at them absently and turn to find Luke right behind me, so close that I feel his breath on my face. Arms crossed over the back of my chair, hat pushed back to reveal dark eyes, lips curved into the hint of a smile, *damn*. I drop the ice cube to the ground and start to straighten the receipt books, afraid that if I stare too long, he'll see the nasty thoughts in my head, what I want him to do to me, what I want to do to him. "Hey," he purrs, ducking his head into his bare arms. His shirt is tied around his waist and his hat brushes against my back. "How's it going up here?"

I shrug. "Okay," I tell him. I glance at Kent, miles away it seems and so damn close, helping an elderly couple carry flats of marigolds to their car. Did they pay for those? Probably gave the money to him, and it's resting in his pocket now with his flask, and that's more profit I'll never add to the deposit, more money for his beer fund. The thought makes me mad all of a sudden and almost bitterly, I sit back in my seat, back against Luke. Crossing my arms, I mutter, "I wish those people would learn to pay *me*. Anything he gets, he just drinks away."

Soft breath tickles my neck, and I look up to see Luke leaning dangerously close to me, mere inches away and I could kiss him now, it'd be that easy, he wants me to, I can see it in his purple gaze. I feel as if I should say something, anything else, but I can't remember how to speak. All I can do is look from his eyes to his mouth, and I don't even mean to lick my lips but I do, just to wet them, he grins at that. "Did you get the crops in?" I ask. I talk to his mouth, I can't look away.

"Most of them," he tells me with an infectious smile that I can't help but return. "I'm taking a break."

A break—sounds good to me. I'd like a break, since I'm obviously not needed here if Kent's going to take payments himself. As I stare at Luke, I think of him naked in the washtub and imagine a few stolen moments... where? Inside the house maybe, tell him I masturbated in his sheets, would that make his grin widen? In my room, in my bed, on the couch, hell in the *kitchen,* anywhere, just so I can taste him again, just so I can feel another's touch, another's lust.

I'd suggest it but from the corner of my eye I see Kent, bending into the trunk of a customer's car, his arms flexing as he lifts the marigold flats. With a quick start, I pull away from Luke, busy myself with straightening the books around the register again, try to ignore the heady scent of his sweat as it envelops me. What the hell am I *thinking*? "Don't let Kent see you," I say. Luke comes around my chair and squats beside me, his arms crossed on the table, his elbow poking at mine, he's that close. "He gets a little pissed if he thinks he's the only one working."

"I'm getting all hot and sweaty," Luke tells me, like he's just making conversation and his words do nothing to me. But he knows what he's doing, it's in his smirk, he knows I'm thinking of him naked now, sheathed in sweat and hot to the touch. He can see it in my eyes, images of me licking the sweat from his body, holding him, thrusting into him until I'm as hot and sticky as he is, and before I can say a word, one hand slips from the table to squeeze my knee. "I guess there's no real hope for another bath tonight, is there?" he asks.

Jesus, no. With Kent home? Never. I fumble for something to say as Luke's hand trails up my thigh, his fingers toying with the inner seam of my jeans. "He bought a showerhead," I say, as if that's the only reason he won't be using the washtub tonight. "Once it's in—"

Luke interrupts me. "That's no fun," he says, and his fingers are pressing against my crotch now, poking at the softness there that quickly hardens to his touch. "I was hoping maybe I could turn the tables tonight, you know?" He speaks low, his words not carrying beyond the two of us, and the customers, the market, Kent, all that's disappeared for me, only Luke remains, his wistful eyes watching his fingers work at the erection rousing in my jeans. "I think you need a little loving, Marcus," he tells me, his fingers rubbing, rubbing at me. "I was just thinking, out there in the field? Lots of time to myself, and I was thinking about what would happen if you crawled in between my sheets tonight, hmm?"

Already did that, I think, my eyes slipping closed as he thumbs along my zipper, presses at me, working me hard through my jeans. "Like, after Kent's asleep, and I'm lying there, and you just happen to come out of your room for say, a drink, or something. And I see you and you see me, and I say come on over here a minute, and I hold my blankets open so you can lie down beside me." I look at him through half-closed eyes, look over at Kent, talking with someone now and ignoring us, and when I look back at Luke, he's smiling at me, his fingers kneading and I tell myself we shouldn't do this but when I grasp his wrist, it's only to hold him closer, not push him away. "Would you do that?" he wants to know. "Would you lie down with me if I asked?"

Speechless, I nod, yes, I would. Who am I kidding? I don't even *have* to be asked, just look at me the right way and I'll trip over my own feet to get to him. "Then I'd touch you here," he murmurs, his fingers easing between my legs, beneath my balls, reaching for the spot where the seams of my jeans meet, the spot that makes my knees weak. "And I'd kiss you—I like your kisses. He still hasn't...?"

"No." The word is a sigh, and I sink down a little in my chair, spread my legs slightly, press my knee against his arm as his fingers continue their gentle massage. I keep looking over at Kent, sure that the moment he glances my way, I'll knock Luke's hand away and sit up, I'll put a stop to this...but he's not looking at us and it's so hard to even think with Luke doing what he's doing to me, I can't imagine telling him to stop. I don't even want to think of Kent right now, or the fact that he still hasn't kissed me yet, or smiled at me, or spoken to me much. Clearing my throat, I run a hand through my ragged hair and moan softly. "Not yet."

"I'll kiss you then," Luke tells me, says *I'll* and not *I'd,* like this is something he's planning to do and not just a daydream anymore. "And I'm real good in the sack, I promise. Last guy I was with couldn't get *enough* of me." No, I imagine he couldn't, not with these hands, those lips, that ass and what I've seen of his cock. If he can work it like he says he can, I'm sure I'll scream out his name when I come. Hell, even if he just lies there, if he gets off on it, on *me,* that'll be more than whatever Kent wants to pretend it is he does when we have sex. "I think you need someone like me, Marcus," Luke is saying, and I agree with him, I think so, too. His fingers in my lap, they convince me I do. "What do you think about that, hmm? Tonight, after he's asleep, you and me—"

"You done out back?"

Kent ducks into the tent and I sit up quickly, cross my legs, inadvertently capturing Luke's hand between my knees. He tugs it free and flashes Kent a disarming grin as he stands. Jesus, I didn't even *see* him come up on us, what's gotten into me? Did he see anything? Did he— "Almost done," Luke says, propping one hand on his hip as he leans over the table and winks at me, *winks,* mother of *God* but he needs to stop that shit. Kent's already nipping at his flask but he has to see what that wink does to me, the flush in my cheeks, the quiver in my hands as I straighten the receipt books again. "Just taking a little break, is all. I'm up to the peppers."

"Jalapeño or banana?" Kent wants to know. He frowns at me but I can't meet his gaze. If I do, he'll see it in my eyes, Luke copping a feel through my jeans, he'll see the desire still smoldering in me if I look at him now.

"I'm not sure?" Luke answers with a shrug. Beneath the table, his foot nudges mine and I stare at the *0.00* display on the register, I'm not looking at either of them, I can't. "Long yellow peppers."

"Those would be banana," Kent tells him, his voice curt, his *no shit, Sherlock* tone. If he were a different man, now would be when he thanks

Luke for helping us, but he doesn't. *If he were different,* I think, frowning at the register tape like it might need to be changed, *then I wouldn't let Luke touch me the way he does, would I?* "Marcus?" Kent asks. I feel my mouth pull into a harsh pout as I glance up at him, only to find him holding out a few folded bills. Nodding at the car in our driveway, he tells me, "The marigolds."

I wonder again if he saw anything before coming into the tent, Luke's hand in my lap, my slack cheeks, my parted lips and half-closed eyes. Taking the offered money, I ring up the purchase and try to think of something to say, it's too quiet between us. "I put the showerhead on the kitchen table," I tell him, it's all that comes to mind. "When you get a chance—"

Kent sighs dramatically. "I've been busy here," he mutters. "Can't just drop everything just to get that done, you know."

"I'll do it," Luke offers. Now I look at him, and he's not watching Kent, he's staring at me. "You say it's in the kitchen?"

I nod and Kent glares at him. "I said I'll take care of it." When he turns his drink-rimmed gaze on me, I shrug halfheartedly. "You want me to do it right this second? You two watch the lot while I rush in there to fix the goddamn shower?"

That *goddamn* makes me shake my head no. Kent's not one to cuss unless he's hitting the hard stuff or pissed to all hell, and I think he's still upset about last night. Hell, *I'm* upset, and it didn't even happen to me. "No," I whisper, I don't want to speak louder, I don't want him to shout. Glancing at Luke, I ask, "Do you know how to put one of those in?"

"Jesus *Christ.*" Kent gives me a look so hard, I'm glad I'm sitting down because it would've dropped me to my seat. "Marcus—"

"I just want it done, okay?" I ask him, getting angry myself. "How hard is it to put a new showerhead in? Five minutes and it's over with, is that asking so much? If Luke can do it—"

Kent turns away. "Fine. You want to do it, kid? Knock yourself out." As he ducks out from under the tent, he adds, "Just don't expect me to come help you, I'm busy here."

Busy, my ass. "I can do it myself," Luke mumbles, and I run a shaky hand across my brow, what the hell's in that flask this early? *Don't take it out on me,* I think, watching Kent's darkened back as he stomps through his plants.

A hand smoothes across my shoulders, soothing, warm. "It's okay," Luke tells me, and I nod, yes, it will be. Once he sleeps this mood of his off, things will be fine. Or rather, as fine as they usually are between us. Quickly, while Kent's back is to us, Luke leans down and kisses the top of my head— I feel his lips through my thick mop of hair, and I almost choke at the stolen gesture.

When he heads for the house, I watch him over my shoulder, memorizing the way his hips sway with each step beneath the shirt that covers his ass and thighs, and I wonder if I could really take him up on his offer tonight, after Kent's asleep. I wonder if I *want* to—

Who am I kidding? I do.

※

KENT ISN'T ONE TO apologize but with Luke gone, I don't feel him watching me so closely, I don't feel his anger simmering when he's nearby. By three in the afternoon, the crowd thins out, more and more time passes between the cars that stop at our stand, and I stretch out in my chair, the fan aimed my way as I stir the air in front of my face with a receipt book. Luke probably got the showerhead up and went back to the vegetables, he'll have the whole field picked over before dinner and Kent will just grumble, he won't even thank the boy, that's just how he is. I'll thank him myself—in my mind I imagine him coming in, sweaty, the beginnings of a burn on his sun-kissed skin, and I'd sit him down in the recliner, climb behind him into the seat, lather his neck and shoulders with Noxzema. I can almost feel the heat of his skin in my hands...

Someone swats at my foot, knocking it off the table, and I sit up as Kent hands me another wad of money. "Look alive, Marcus," he tells me, squinting at the empty road. The last car pulled out of our lot almost a half hour ago. "Slow today."

"Just a little." I ring up a no-sale and stuff the money into the register, aware of Kent standing so close to me. It's his way of saying things are cool between us again, because if he was still mad, he'd just storm off. I think whatever's in that flask of his is gone now, and it's mellowed him out a bit, alcohol does that to him. A little and he's almost willing to smile, almost—I think if I try hard enough, I might be able to make him grin.

Because we're dead, I start counting the money out, why not? I'm sure we won't get much more business today. Fingering the dingy bills, I hope I sound nonchalant when I ask, "How much of the deposit yesterday actually made it into the bank?"

"Most of it," he says, evasive. He had that extra twenty in his pocket, so I know he didn't use a lot of it for drink, but the bail had to be a pretty penny. "A hundred fifty," he tells me before I ask.

"You put that in?" I want to know. There was a *hell* of a lot more money than that in yesterday's bag. If he just put in a hundred fifty dollars—

But Kent shakes his head. "That's what they charged me." He doesn't say it was the police and I don't mention the incident, but it hangs between us like a loaded gun, waiting to go off and shatter this uneasy peace. "Plus seventy-five to get the bumper hammered out, and fifty at the store." Seeing my frown, he says, "I put most of it in the bank, don't worry."

I don't answer. *Most of it* isn't all. I don't ask how much he spent at the bar and he doesn't offer the information up. What do I care? It's his money, his business, his damn plants, let him waste what he wants, it's none of *my* concern. I'm just trying to help him out here. I'm just trying to keep his finances straight because I'm good with numbers. As long as *I* have a roof over my head, food on my table, what is it to me?

A rough arm snakes around my waist, and I take an involuntary gulp of fresh air before Kent pulls me to him. He reeks of sweat and tequila, so that's what he's been at all day. Shoving the money into a deposit bag, I try to be diplomatic as I tell him, "Luke fixed the shower, baby. Maybe you might want to clean up before dinner?" He sighs against my neck like the thought of washing himself is a huge inconvenience, and I elbow him playfully. I think of Luke and his kisses, his hands, and it's guilt that makes me add, "Maybe I'll join you. What do you say?"

He laughs into my skin. "So that's why you wanted it fixed, hmm?" His hand slips down to paw at me through my jeans, a clumsy squeeze that still manages to turn me on. "You could've said so."

Yeah, like my telling him I want sex has ever gotten me far before. Still, he rubs against me and I push Luke out of my mind, this is my lover, this man, this cowboy here, and I've made him smile, I've turned him on, we have to grab this moment quick. So I follow him to the house, and thank God Luke's still out back, I don't want to see him right this minute, I'm sure he'd look at me and know what we're going to do, and I'd feel the need to apologize…for what? For wanting to have sex with Kent? Or because it's not with *him*?

I'm not sure.

In the bathroom, the new showerhead's in place and the tiny room is cramped with the both of us, so I stand out in the hall and undress. Part of me *hopes* Luke comes in and sees this, sees me, naked and half-hard and maybe he'd tell us to stop, maybe he'd say he loves me and doesn't want me with Kent, like at a wedding when they ask if anyone has objections, and then what?

Maybe they'd *both* go at me, God what a thought, it makes me want to come just *thinking* that, two guys at once, I've seen it in pornos but never had it myself. Kent behind me because he doesn't like it up the ass and Luke in front, I'd hold him up against the wall, I'd kiss him while Kent shoved into me and he'd be so tight around my cock, so hot, so *sweet.* Seeing my erection stiffen, Kent laughs as he turns on the shower. Water splashes the tiles and the curtain squeals as he pulls it across the bar. "Did you miss me?" he asks with a slap on my ass.

I grin. Let him think that but to be honest? It's the thought of kissing Luke that turns me on right now, not Kent in me but me in someone else, that boy outside, me loving *him,* that's going to get me off. Still, I can't say Kent does nothing for me, that's a lie, and when he strips out of his clothes and I get a glimpse of his own pale erection, I'm eager for him. He climbs into the shower and I step into the bathroom, close the door, already massaging my balls as I slip into the shower.

Kent takes me from behind, that's the way he likes to do it. I grip the towel rack in front of me and moan as loud as I dare—I like the echo off the walls of the shower, I like the water beating on my back, his hands on my hips and his hard dick pressing into me, in my mind it's Luke shoving in harder, faster, *harder* and deeper. It's Luke's hands that rub at my pelvis, his fingers that encircle my shaft, his nails that scrape across my balls and when I come, it's his name I have to bite back. And still he drives into me, he works me hard again, he tugs at my dick and moans my name in Kent's voice. *Kent...*

That jars the fantasy. With a guilty start I realize I'm with him, not the boy in my dreams, *Kent,* and almost as if I'm trying to make up for thinking of Luke, I push against him, my muscles tightening to keep him in, to get him off, I don't want him to even *think* it wasn't him in my mind, it wasn't him who made me come. "Kent," I moan, just to chase away the visions that cling to me, Luke's hands and his lips and his tight ass, his thick cock. "Jesus, Kent, *please.*"

Tighter, harder, faster, and finally he pulls out of me, almost exhausted, and I feel him spurt against my buttocks, rancid, alcoholic cum but it's more than he's managed in a long time, it's hot and fast and enough to get me off again. "Kent," I sigh, as his hands wipe his juices from me. Turning, I pick at one of his nipples and ask coyly, "Did you miss *me?*"

He swats my hand away. "You know you have a great ass," he tells me. That's what he always says after we fuck, and I like it because it's the closest he's ever come to telling me that *I'm* great. I should mention it to Luke, just to hear the boy say that if I were his, he'd tell me stuff like that out of the blue. *I'd say I love you all the time,* I can almost hear the words in his voice, they tug at the sudden weight between my legs and I pull Kent to me, water cascading down around us like rain. "Kiss me," I say, because I want him to, I want him to hold me like Luke did last night, his arms rubbing my back, his lips insistent on mine. My mouth finds his chin, his cheek, his upper lip. I sigh into him and taste the bittersweet tequila that stains his breath and takes mine away.

But he pulls back. "Marcus," he complains, reaching for the shampoo. I get the feeling he doesn't like to kiss because he doesn't really know how—I'd offer to teach him but he'd just say he doesn't like it, we already did the deed, why bother fooling around anymore? He doesn't get the whole afterplay thing that I like, the cuddling and touching and sucking and kissing, he thinks it's a waste of time. "We just did it," he tells me, soaping up his hair. "You came twice. Don't tell me you want it again."

Is that so bad? To hear him tell it, yeah, and so he won't see me pout, I step out of the shower, I guess I'm finished here then. "Never mind," I tell him, wrapping a towel around my waist.

"Marcus," he sighs, like I'm being petulant and unreasonable. I pull the curtain closed so I won't have to see him roll his eyes. "Maybe later, what do you say?"

I say you'll be too drunk by then, I think, but I don't say it out loud. Instead I shrug as I towel off and tell him, "Sure." As if he won't be asleep later. Whatever.

I leave him to finish showering and step out into the hall, the shadows cool on my drying skin after the heat of the water. I'm all too aware of my naked chest above the towel at my waist, my naked legs below. I wonder if Luke's in yet, if he's sitting in the living room and waiting for us to finish up, if he's thinking about me.

But the living room is empty, I see that from the hall before I duck into my room, and maybe it's better this way, that he doesn't know. Then I won't feel like I have to apologize when I see him, I won't have to look into his violet eyes and see…what? Indignation, desire, anger? I'm not sure, though I know what I'd *like* to see there, staring back at me. I'd like to see that lust shining in his eyes again, I'd like to taste his kisses—in the tub yesterday, he didn't pull away after he got off, he wanted to keep kissing me, he wanted more. What would that be like, to hold someone close instead of being pushed away? To lie down after sex with another instead of always being alone?

In my room, I kick at the door to close it and drop the towel. The door doesn't shut completely and I don't care—let Kent see me like this, he's still in the bathroom. Let *Luke* see me like this, walk past my room and get a glimpse of *my* body, and then we *could* close the door, he could lay me down on my bed and damn but I shouldn't think shit like this, I shouldn't even

Cowboy 57

dream of fooling around on Kent—

A single red gerbera daisy lies on my pillow.

Tentatively I pick up the flower. I bury my nose in the soft petals and just smell pollen. A *flower.* For all his plants, Kent's never given me anything like this before. The agave in the corner, that's it, but it doesn't bloom, it's not the color of love, it's not *this.*

So he was in here. While I was in the shower with Kent, Luke was in my room. Did he lie down on my bed? Press his head back against my pillow, twirl the flower between his fingers and wait for me? These walls are thin—did he hear me moan? Did he hear Kent's quick grunts, my breathless gasps? Does he realize it was him in there with me in my mind, that it wasn't Kent who got me off but *him*? God, how could I ever tell him *that*?

I dress quickly, ashamed. He makes me feel like this, like I've cheated on him, on *him* and he's not even my lover, how does he *do* this to me? There's a cup on my bedside table, still half-full with drinking water, and I stick the flower in there, turn it until the daisy is aimed at my pillow. When I lie down I'll be able to look into the red petals, I'll think of Luke when I see it. As I leave my room, I pull the door shut so Kent can't see the flower when he passes—he's still in the shower, though, I hear him—and I head down the hall.

Luke's in the kitchen. As I enter, he looks up from where he sits at the table cutting vegetables. He grins at me and I don't see anything in his eyes or his smile that tells me he's mad. "Pepper steak," he says, pushing his chair back as he stands. "I just had a hankering for some, you know?"

"Don't let Kent see you pick his flowers," I say. I could slap myself— no thank you? *I don't want to encourage him,* I tell myself. Bullshit.

But his grin widens. "You like it?" he asks. Before I can reply, he steps around the table and kisses the corner of my mouth. "Is he still in there?" he whispers.

When I nod, he leans forward and this time his lips find mine, his tongue parting them easily, and he's as sweet as I remember, his breath more intoxicating than Kent's without the alcohol. "I'm sorry," I sigh, squeezing my eyes shut against sudden tears. "Luke, I'm so sorry, I thought of you the whole time—"

"Shh," he murmurs, kissing me again. "It's okay, Marcus, I understand. Do you like the flower?"

I rub at my eyes, I'm so damn *tired.* Of this charade, these two men, my own body that seeks to betray us all. "I love it," I tell him. "I can't be doing this, Luke. I love *him*—"

Luke kisses me again. "Are you sure it's him?" he asks as his arms slip around my waist, "and not just someone you think he is? One of those guys in your magazines, maybe?"

I like it here in his arms, with his lips and hands on me, the sound of the shower as distant as rain. "I don't know," I admit.

❈

OVER DINNER, KENT DOESN'T thank Luke, no surprise there. He sits at the head of the table, bent over his plate, eyes beginning to droop—the alcohol is getting to him, the sex, he'll take a nap after this. "Good peppers," he says, glancing at me. I nod, yes, very good. "Onions are real sweet this year. I told you it was a good idea to keep them in the back field, didn't I?"

I nod again and smile across the table at Luke, who frowns at his plate until he sees me look his way, then grins to beat the sun. Leave it to Kent to focus on his own efforts in the garden and not even thank the cook. "It's really good," I tell Luke. "How do you get the meat so tender?"

Suddenly Luke's bare foot finds my crotch beneath the table, and with a wink, he digs his toes into the pillowy softness of my genitals, already hardening beneath his touch. "You just have to beat it right," he says, smiling.

I had to ask, didn't I? In front of Kent, too, *Jesus*. But my lover doesn't look up from his plate, doesn't see the look Luke's giving me, doesn't know about the foot in my lap. "It's all in how you prepare it," Kent mutters.

Does he even realize that we're not talking about the steak here?

I have to duck my head to keep from smirking, and beneath the table, my hand covers Luke's toes, my fingers lacing between them and squeezing gently. Kent looks at me, at Luke who nods encouragingly, and back at me again. "You could do this, Marcus," he says, pointing a fork at his plate. "You just rush it too fast. Hit it a few times before you stick it in—" Luke's toes curl down in my hand and I can't stop the laugh that interrupts Kent. "Did I say something funny?" he wants to know, his voice hard with drink.

"No," I mumble. I push Luke's foot away and say it again, "No," shaking my head so Kent will believe me. "Sorry, babe. I didn't mean…" No excuse comes to mind, so I attack my food with renewed vigor and refuse to look at either of them. "Sorry."

For a long, breathless moment, I don't think he's going to let it drop. He's been hitting the worm, it makes him mean-spirited, I hate the tequila more than the beer or the whiskey or anything else he drinks. He's still a little touchy about last night, and he thinks I'm smarting him right now, I don't want a fight—

Cowboy

Apparently, neither does he.

Another look at Luke, who shrugs as if he doesn't know what's gotten into me, that minx, and Kent turns back to his dinner. The rest of the meal is eaten in strained silence. I think I should apologize again but it'll just set Kent off on how it's disrespectful to laugh at the table, when he's talking no less, and I don't want a lecture right now. What I *want* is Luke's foot back in between my thighs, his toes in my hand, his heel grinding into the erection budding in my jeans, but I can't catch his eye, he doesn't look at me again. Finally, Kent pushes back from the table and belches as he stands. "Good peppers," he says again. That's as close to a complement on his cooking that Luke's going to get.

Kent doesn't bother to take his plate to the sink. Instead, he opens the fridge for a beer—just what he needs, I'm sure—and tells us, "Be outside." He opens the screen door, clomps out on the porch, and is gone.

Now Luke looks at me, a self-satisfied smirk on his face, and his foot is back in my lap again, poking and prodding and piquing my interest. "Don't even," I warn before he can make some off-color comment, but even that's enough to make us both giggle into our plates. *See what you do to me?* I think, shaking my head. "You're going to get me in trouble," I tell him.

His toes curl into my crotch. "Me?" he asks innocently. "You're doing a good job of that yourself. Who was it that started this whole thing, hmm?" When I frown at him, he raises an eyebrow and asks, "Yesterday? In the washtub? Or didn't you mean that?"

I can't reply. I meant it, I want it again—he's right, I *am* getting into trouble here, I'm rushing headlong into danger, flirting with him and wanting him and *thinking* of him when I fuck Kent, he should just leave. Let me get back to who I thought I was, let me love the man I thought I loved...*but you know you won't let him go,* a voice inside whispers, and that's the truth. If Luke said he had to leave now? I'd do anything to stop him, to keep him here with me. I'm falling in love with *him,* too. "You kiss me like you mean it," he says softly.

I meet his amethyst eyes, then drop my gaze to his mouth, his chest, his hands. "I do," I admit. *There, you happy? I said it, I mean it, I do.*

"You thought of me?" he asks. "When you guys were—"

I don't want to hear the words in his voice. "I told you I did." Pushing back from the table, I pick up Kent's plate and my own. I turn towards the sink, away from Luke, away from those eyes and those hands and that mouth. "I don't really want to talk about it?" I ask as I run the water. I don't talk louder than the rush from the spigot. "If you don't mind. When it's just you and me, I don't want to think about...about him. Please."

"Okay." I hear the clatter of silverware then the scrape of his chair, he comes around the table to the sink, and his arm eases around my waist as he slips his plate into the water with the others. His hand strums my stomach, his lips kiss the tender skin behind my ear. "I like to be licked," he breathes, out of nowhere, and beneath his fingers, my stomach flips nervously; lower, my groin starts to ache like a rotten tooth, a steady throb I want him to alleviate. "That little place below your nuts, the taint? Cause it ain't ass and it ain't dick, you know where I mean?"

I look out the kitchen window—Kent's in his market, throwing tarp over the stands, tying down the tent, stopping now and then to swig at his beer—and my throat clicks audibly when I swallow, I know exactly where Luke means. I imagine my tongue there, the sweaty musk of his scent sharp in my senses, his thighs cradling my head and his hands in my hair. I could make him cry by just licking him, I'm sure of it, my lips kissing quivering skin, my teeth nipping playfully, my tongue rimming him until he *sobs* my name...

"I want you *there*, Marcus," he purrs as he rubs my stomach, and his other hand cups the hardness trapped in my jeans. With a nod at the window, he wants to know, "What's *he* taste like? Is he sweet like me? Is he firm?"

I shake my head. Kent? "He's not into that," I whisper. My voice sounds foreign to my own ears, a ragged scrape like sandpaper. I've never licked Kent before. I'm sure he tastes like beer, though, alcohol seeps from his pores, and he's getting paunchy, doesn't exercise—*firm* isn't a word that comes to mind. I'm sure he's nothing like this boy holding me now, nothing at all.

"Are *you*?" Luke murmurs, his lips on my ear, one hand on my stomach, the other on my cock. I can't breathe with him this close—if I ever got the courage to take him up on his offer, I don't know how I'd go through with it, I'd die to see him stretched out before me, naked, glorious, *mine*. But he's persistent, and his tongue licks out to taste me, his lips close over my earlobe, and he asks, "When's the last time he licked you?"

Never, I think. I don't have to admit it, though, Luke already knows—in the way my hands shake and my lower lip trembles as he kisses me. "You want me to," he sighs. It's not a question.

I don't answer him, because I do.

※

It takes another three beers to put Kent out. We're in the living room, all three of us, the TV on and Kent in his recliner, his chin drooping to his chest every so often. Luke sits at one end of the couch and I'm at the other, his pillow between us like a line of demarcation neither wants to cross. Not while Kent's still up, more or less. Not while he's sitting right here.

I don't know what we're watching—I stare at the screen but don't see it. Instead my eyes burn with the images in my mind, Luke on this couch and me above him, both of us naked and hard, my hands and lips making him moan and buck against me. In the vision, Kent's asleep in the recliner and that just fuels the fire inside me, the knowledge that at any moment he'll open his eyes and see me going down on Luke, it's enough to make me hurt with lust, and I have to cross my legs to hide the erection swelling in my pants.

I clear my throat, glance around at the others, Luke watching TV and Kent staring into the bottom of his beer mug as if he's thinking he might just have one more before calling it a night, but they don't look at me, they don't know the sordid thoughts swirling through my head.

Thank God. I wonder if Luke's thinking the same things, if he's only pretending to watch TV like I am and he's really seeing the two of us clasped together in throes of passion. Things I shouldn't be thinking. I'm not like this, honest. I'm not one to fuck around on someone, I'm not the type to fall for the first cute guy I see, I'm *not*.

But it's been so long since anyone's looked at me the way Luke does, how did he put it? *It's a hard look to deny.* No shit. If Kent even *thought* about speaking to me the way Luke does, I wouldn't dream of running around on him. If he said half the things Luke's told me, if he looked at me with the same desire in his eyes, there would be no need for the boys in the magazine ads beneath my bed. I had almost forgotten that those words, those glances, that much need and desire could exist in another, could be directed towards *me*. How can I not want that?

A startled snort disrupts my thoughts and I look over at Kent to see him shaking himself awake. Something akin to pity makes me tell him, "Why don't you get on to bed?"

Luke frowns at Kent as he rouses himself. "I'm fine," he mutters, his voice slurred. But when he reaches for his empty mug, he hits it with the back of his hand, sends it tumbling to the floor. "Shit."

"Come on," I say, standing. When Kent pushes the recliner into an upright position, I take his arm and tug gently. "You're tired, babe. Long day. I'll help you to your room."

He's heavy but I get him to his feet and as he leans against me, I stagger beneath his weight. "Marcus," he murmurs, his hands fisting in my shirt, and despite the shower, he still smells of sweat and booze. His breath is like a furnace against my neck. "My cup—"

"I've got it," Luke says, reaching over the arm of the couch for the mug on the floor. "You go on. Night, Kent. Thanks for everything."

Kent mumbles something about the rest of the crop, I can't make out his words, he's already half-asleep, but Luke nods and tells him, "Sure, man. We'll knock that out tomorrow, what do you say? A good night's sleep and we'll hit the fields first thing, you got it."

Kent stumbles for the hall, dragging me along behind him. Luke's good at this, isn't he? Saying all the right things, nodding in the right places—he's had practice, what with his dad like this, he knows how it is. Anything to get through the drunken times and see the sober man beneath the alcohol again. In the darkened hall, I smooth my hands along Kent's hot back and whisper, "Look at yourself." Kent gurgles, a noncommittal noise in the back of his throat. Suddenly he seems older than he is, he seems ancient and weary and sad, so damn sad. *I do this to him,* I think, holding the door to his room open as he shuffles to the bed. He's this way because of me. I'm not as good as I can be, I'm not as good as he says I am, if only I was so much more, he wouldn't have to drink himself stupid every single night—

You're not the reason he does what he does, a voice whispers in my mind, and it's Luke. I push his words away as my fingers fumble over Kent's belt in the darkness. I try not to think of that boy in the other room as I unzip my lover's jeans and pull them down legs that are pale in the moonlight seeping through the slit in the curtains. At the foot of the bed, I tug off Kent's boots, toss them aside, then pull off his jeans completely, flip the covers up over his naked legs.

"Get some sleep, hon," I murmur, kissing his forehead, but he's already out, the first ragged snores rumbling through him. His hat I hang on the bedpost, near his head so he can find it in the morning, and I prop his boots up in front of the door before I pull it shut—I'll hear him trip over them if he gets up later. *Just in case,* I tell myself. The last thing I want is him in the hall, heading for the bathroom, while Luke and I are on the couch…

I won't even *think* about what it is we might do, I shouldn't think it, I should just close Kent's door and head into my own room, jerk off in my bed if I have to, anything to keep me from returning to the living room and the boy there who I know is waiting for me. I have a lover, passed out in a drunken stupor. I shouldn't *need* anyone else—

But I do.

Quietly I close the door on Kent's snores and tiptoe down the hall, as if afraid of waking him. I just need kisses, that's all I'm thinking of as I hurry

Cowboy

to the living room, Luke's mouth on mine, his soft lips, his insistent tongue and maybe his hands beneath my clothing, that'll be enough for me. Something Kent doesn't give me, is that asking too much? As long as it's not *sex,* it's not really cheating, right?

Luke's already stretched out along the couch, the TV off, the pillow moved to one end beneath his head. His shirt's unbuttoned, exposing his smooth chest, hairless, muscular. At his waist, his jeans are unzipped, his boxers open, his balls and cock hanging through the gapping fabric like a promise. He's already hard, and for the first time I get a good look at him, he's a healthy size, seven inches, maybe eight, and red and thick and beautiful. Not much hair, either, he must shave it off, it makes him look impossibly young and stirs me more than I'd like to admit—Kent's dark hair stains his skin like ink, it makes him look whiter than he really is, but Luke has a downy fuzz that catches the light and winks golden when I move closer, like spider webs or gossamer thread. One hand props his head up as he watches me with hooded eyes, and the other rubs along the length of his shaft, stroking lightly. "He asleep?" he wants to know.

I don't trust myself to speak so I simply nod, yes, asleep. Reaching out, Luke takes my hand, guides me to the side of the couch, pokes at my crotch. "You wanna play a little bit?" he asks, a coy smile on his lips. Before I can answer, he's already working my zipper down, picking at me through the thin material of my boxers. "He won't be getting up any time soon, will he?"

Kent. He's talking about Kent, my lover, but I can't seem to care about that now, not with his hand in my pants, his fingers on me. "He usually sleeps through the night," I say as Luke cradles my balls. I gasp as he extracts them from my shorts, my hard length pointing at him, I have to lean over and grip the back of the couch at the sensation. Kent's hands aren't this tender, this loving, *ever.*

"Lie down," Luke tells me, patting the couch beside him, and I do as I'm told, on my side like he is and facing him. His lips touch mine in a sweet kiss while his arm wraps around my waist, pulls me to him, crushes our erections together with an eagerness I haven't felt in years.

I'm reminded of when I was thirteen and so in love with the boy next door, Pete Buckler, older than me, who knew I had the worst crush on him, he'd prance around in his swim trunks and let me watch him swim laps around his family's pool. Luke makes me feel the same way Pete did, heady and young and *alive.* Once Pete even called me over, asked if I wanted to swim with him, and he worked me into the deep end, up against the side of the pool. The water was cold around my legs and I was scared, terrified because I couldn't touch the bottom. Then Pete pulled down his trunks, pulled down mine, and pressed his naked body against me.

For the first time I felt another boy's skin against mine, I felt a hard dick and soft balls and I held the sides of the pool in a death grip while Pete whispered that it was okay, it's alright, his hand beneath the water stroking us both until I came. He kept against me, trying to get off, moaning into my face, until his mother yelled out the window, *Get off that boy, Pete, 'fore you drown him!* She thought we were horsing around is all, boys being boys, but Pete kissed me clumsily before he ripped my shorts away completely, a quick peck on the corner of my lips, my first kiss. Then he tossed my shorts out of the pool and laughed as I scrambled out naked to get them.

But Luke's kisses aren't clumsy or inexpert. His hands know what they're doing, caressing my back and ass, slipping between us to squeeze at our erections, thumbing over my chest and stomach. His legs move along mine, his knee rising between my thighs to push against me. His mouth is hungry, his lips tender, his moans soft and almost indistinct as we rub together. If Kent came out now, he'd see us, and even if I heard him trip over his boots, I wouldn't stop this, I *couldn't*, I want it too much, need it, need *Luke*. I don't want this moment to end.

It's over too quick. Luke moves against me, humping back against the couch, arching into me, his hand working between us, and I can feel him shudder in release as he kisses me, my name on his lips. A hot dampness coats my erection and I rise up on my elbow, thrust into his cum-slicked hand, gasp his name into the hollow of his throat as I get off. "Jesus," I sigh into him, thrusting slowly, I like the feel of him on me.

"He had nothing to do with it," Luke jokes. He smears my lower belly with our juices, kisses my chin when I laugh. And when I snuggle against him, I think that this is what I'm missing with Kent, right here, these arms around me, this voice whispering silly things in my ear.

❋

I WAKE TO LUKE'S flower staring down at me from the glass on my bedside table. A ray of bright sun catches one petal, turning the red into a brilliant hue, the color of a heart in full bloom. *I love him,* I think suddenly, and because it's so unexpected, I know it's true. I love that boy asleep on the couch in the living room, love him completely, and I'll never be the same again. I won't let him leave me. I wouldn't be able to live without him.

Stretching languidly, I feel the covers move over my naked skin and remember the few stolen moments we shared last night, after Kent went to bed. I remember kisses, Luke's mouth on mine, his hand encircling me. I remember his soft words, breathless giggles, kisses, touches, *love*. Last night was something more than all the sex I've ever had with Kent, it was something deeper, something meaningful, and penetration wasn't even a part of that. The two of us on the couch, holding each other tight? *That* was making love, those half-whispered sighs, those tender kisses. *That* was something I've never felt with Kent, and it was so wonderful and amazing that I don't think anything else can ever compare to the way I felt in Luke's embrace.

With a contented sigh, I stretch my arms above my head and smile at his flower. I can almost picture him stirring on the couch, maybe his blankets falling to the floor, a slight chill creeping in around his legs and arms. I imagine he's cold, and Kent's outside at the market already, watering the plants he cares for more than me. Half-asleep, an ache like the heel of a foot pressing into his bladder, Luke would tumble from the couch, down the hall, stand in the darkness of the bathroom with closed eyes as he relieves himself. Then, on the way back, he'd notice my door ajar. Push it open just enough to peek inside and see me lying here like an invitation. Slip into my room, close the door behind him, pad barefoot to my bed and crawl beneath my covers, cuddling up to me in the early morning light. I'd hold him as he fell back asleep…

"Marcus!"

Kent's voice shatters my daydream and stuns me awake. I hear the *clomp clomp* of his heavy boots on the hardwood floor, and then he calls out again, closer this time, from the end of the hall. "You getting up sometime today?" he wants to know.

Fuck. Those boots down the hall, heading towards me, he stops in front of my door and knocks, like I could've possibly slept through his hollering. "Marcus," he starts.

"I'm up." I throw the covers off me as I stumble to my feet. My jeans are on the floor—I tug them on over my boxers and say it again when Kent jiggles the door knob. I don't want him coming in and seeing the flower. "I'm up, babe."

He doesn't answer, just turns and stomps away, and when I open the door, the hall is empty. I hear Luke's voice from the kitchen, he asks if I'm awake, and Kent's reply is an unintelligible grunt. What time is it? Still early, if he's not outside. Waiting for his coffee then, or something to eat. I hope he doesn't expect me—

The heavenly smell of frying bacon fills my senses as I step into the living room. "What's cooking?" I ask, coming into the kitchen. Luke stands at the stove, dressed in my clothes and scrambling eggs while Kent sits in his chair, no shirt on, his hat cocked back. Walking around behind him, I pluck the hat off his head and set it on the table.

When he looks up at me, I plant a quick kiss on his forehead. He rolls his eyes and says, "You sleep too damn much, Marcus."

"Morning to you, too," I grumble. I'd like to sidle up behind Luke now, ease an arm around his waist, kiss *him,* but I settle for a secretive brush of my hand against the small of his back as I pour myself a cup of coffee. Lowering my voice, I murmur, "Hey."

Luke laughs and bumps my hip with his. "Hey, lazybones. Sleep well?"

Blowing on the hot java, I look at him over the top of the mug. "Like a baby," I tell him, keeping my voice quiet. At the table, Kent's shaking out the daily newspaper, ignoring us, and I feel brazen enough to wink at Luke. "What about you?" He laughs again. "What?" I ask, grinning slowly.

Leaning close, he whispers, "Did you dream of me?"

I glance at Kent, nose buried in the paper—can he hear us? Does he care? With a quick gulp of scalding coffee, I admit, "Some." His eyes light up, an amazing shade of lavender that I swear I've seen in Kent's garden as the sun sets, and before he can ask for details, I nudge him with my hip to keep him quiet, then take my seat. Not with Kent right *here.* Damn.

The milk is on the table—I pour as much as I can into my coffee, until the cup threatens to overflow. Kent doesn't look at me, doesn't say a word, so I stare into the muddy drink and stir it slowly with my spoon, waiting for something to break the silence. Is this how it is between us now? After two years together, we have nothing to say? Just a frantic fuck in the shower, a few curt words over dinner, that's it?

Luke sets a plate in front of me, eggs and bacon and toast. "Thanks," I murmur into the food—I don't look at him, don't want Kent to see the lust in my eyes or hear the desire in my voice, so I dive into the eggs and pretend the boy standing so close does nothing to me. I can ignore the ache in my groin, the heat in my blood. I *have* to.

But he makes it so hard when he leans against me to set a plate down before Kent, and his hip presses into my arm, a slight erection poking my elbow. And he does it again, leaning into me to set out his own plate across the table. I feel him staring at me, willing me to look up and see his smile, his eyes, but I don't. I concentrate on the heat that rises from my eggs and coffee, instead.

We eat in the silence that envelops us like summer sun, searing our skin and draining our energy, until I feel exhausted and worn down from simply sitting between these two men. Luke keeps glancing at me but I don't meet his eyes, and when I look at Kent, he doesn't look up from his plate. There's a part of me that wants to cry out in frustration, scream, shout, *anything* to break through this meniscus of mediocrity that threatens to smother us all. I want *some* kind of reaction—tell Kent how I feel for Luke, what would he say? Would he get angry, get mad?

Or would he just shrug in that way he has that makes me think he's not even hearing what I say?

What would Luke do or say if I mentioned the dreams I had last night, him in my arms and me in him? Would he want to hear more, maybe live out the scenes in my mind? Or would he nod at Kent as if to tell me *not here, not now*? Am I the only one who feels this pressure building around us? Am I the only one here who feels like he's going to explode?

Just as I'm about to say something—mention the flower, maybe that'll get a rise from them—Kent mumbles into his eggs. "Want you in the barn today," he says, and I glance across the table at Luke, staring back at me. Which one of us is he talking to?

When he gets no response, Kent looks up at me. "You hear me?" he asks.

"Me?" I want to know. "The barn? What for?"

Kent turns back to his food. "Needs cleaning out," he tells me. He knows I hate that barn. "Hay all over the damn place. Shouldn't take long."

But why me? "I'm on the register," I remind him. "Kent, you know how I feel about—"

"Nothing dead in there," he interrupts, and the look he gives me stems any other argument I might have. "I went in this morning, Marcus. I'll take care of the payments today, you just get that hay up."

Send Luke, I think, frowning into my plate. Suddenly I'm not hungry anymore, and I have to force myself to swallow the eggs in my mouth, dry as sawdust, they scrape my throat on the way down. The hay is Luke's mess— he tore open a bundle when he spent the night out there, threw that shit all over the stall. Let *him* clean it up, not me. "You hear me?" Kent asks again.

I push my chair back and stand up so quick that it knocks against the stove, rocks back on two legs, threatens to fall but doesn't. "I hear you," I growl, pissed. Picking up my plate, I turn from the table so they can't see my shaking hands, and as I scrape the rest of my eggs into the trash, I say bitterly, "I know you too well, Kent. Any money you get today won't go in that register and you know it. You'll pocket the cash and when you ride into town, you'll use it to get shit-faced all over again. And then what? You got lucky once but what happens if you hit a tree the next time you're too damn drunk to drive home? What happens if you kill yourself?"

I feel his rage like a caged animal, snarling at me even though he doesn't say a word. Angry myself, I throw my dish into the sink, my silverware, my cup, and what's left of my coffee splashes the stainless steel before spiraling away down the drain. *Fuck him,* I think. If he doesn't care enough about himself, doesn't care enough about *me,* then fuck him to hell. I tell myself I just don't care.

Luke watches me as I storm around the table, behind his chair so Kent can't reach out and grab my wrist, I don't want him touching me. I'll clean the goddamn barn, fine. Let him steal from his own profits, *fine.*

Down the hall, into my room, I slam the door behind me hard enough to rattle the window. Too hard—it pops back open an inch, I can hear Kent's boots echoing towards me. "*Fuck* you," I cry out.

The words come unbidden, tear through me like knives, slash at my body and I hope he hears them, I don't care anymore. I kick at the door to close it, hear the slap of wood on flesh, and Kent pushes his way into my room. His eyes are hard glints below his damn cowboy hat, and his lips are twisted in a sour scowl. "What the hell is your problem today?" he wants to know.

"Get out," I tell him. He reaches for me but I pull away. "Don't fucking touch me, Kent. Get the hell out of my room." Before he can reply, I tear open my closet, yank down the first shirt I grab, shrug into it without looking at him or his reflection in the mirror above my dresser. "You don't sleep here," I mutter. "You never wanted to come in here before. Don't start now."

"What's this all about?" Kent asks. His voice is hard, and from the corner of my eye I see him, arms crossed, blocking the door because he's in the mood for a fight and I'm not getting out of this snit so easily. He'll want an apology—he's that way, can't say sorry himself but damned if he doesn't want to hear it for the littlest slight against *him.* "Marcus—"

Then he notices the flower on my table, the gerbera daisy that Luke picked for me, and I swear I see his already sunburnt face turn a darker shade of red. "I thought I told you about this shit," he says, nodding at the cup of water and its inhabitant. The stem is already starting to droop. "*This* is our livelihood, Marcus. You pick one flower and that's one less plant I can sell."

"One less beer you can drink," I counter. *And I didn't pick it,* I think—I should tell him that. *Luke did, he picked it for me so there.* Only then he'll get mad at Luke, he's just looking for trouble today and if he turns his gaze on the boy, he's likely to kick him out and I don't want that. Right now Luke's the only thing keeping me from shoving my handful of clothes into a pillowcase and hitting the road. *Then what will you do?* I want to know, watching Kent watch me. *If I leave your sorry ass, what'll happen to you then?*

I expect an outburst, maybe a swing of his fist—he hasn't hit me before but there's always a first time, right? And he has a little buzz on, I know that wasn't just coffee in his mug. Hell, he's probably still drunk from last night.

So the last thing I'm ready for is the defeated sigh, the hand that rubs at his eyes, the soft voice that asks, "This is about the other night, isn't it? When I…"

He trails off, unable to say it. *When I slept off the booze in jail.* "Marcus," he murmurs, and this time when he reaches for me, I don't pull away. His arms come up around my shoulders, he hugs me close, presses my head against his shoulder and I can feel his heart beat in time with my own, I can smell the sickening sweet scent of alcohol rise from his naked skin. But his hands are so strong, so gentle, and his chest is a solid wall I can't fight against, I just let him crush me in his embrace, my arms limp at my sides, his hand mussing my hair. "I didn't mean to scare you," he says, still speaking low. He rubs my back like he's trying to cheer me up. "I'm—don't be like this. It won't happen again, I swear."

I don't answer. Of course it won't happen—he's going to court for that little mishap, isn't he? And he'll lose his license, I'll have to drive him into town, he'll get as drunk as he wants because he knows I'll drive him home. I'm well aware of the fact that he still hasn't said he's sorry. "Marcus?" He kisses my forehead, a rough press of damp lips that leaves a smear I want to wipe away. "Just work with me here, please, that's all I'm asking. I'll keep count of the sales and give you all the money for the deposit."

"It's not about the fucking money," I say, pushing away from him. I slip out of his arms easily—he just lets me go. "Jesus, Kent. You could've been killed. Doesn't that *mean* anything to you?" When I see the confused look on his face, I hug myself and turn away. "You'd think it'd be a wake-up call, babe," I tell him, my anger still clinging to me. "A sort of maybe I shouldn't drink so much, you know?"

The edge is back in his voice. "I can handle myself," he says. "I took my eyes off the road for two seconds, Marcus. It could've happened to anyone…"

"It happened to *you*." I glance at him over my shoulder, see the hard eyes, the set mouth, and I know this isn't getting through to him. He's not an alcoholic, not *him*. "Forget it," I mutter. His hand touches my shoulder and I shrug it off. "Leave me alone. I've got a barn to clean, remember?"

I push past him towards the door. "I'll give you the damn money," he says as he trails behind me.

"Keep your money," I tell him. I shake my shirt on to settle it over my shoulders, my fingers fumbling with the buttons. Luke stands in the doorway between the kitchen and living room, a slight frown on his face—I glance at him, see the hurt in his eyes, and have to look away as I shove through the screen door and out into the backyard, Kent on my heels. Ahead, the barn looms ominous, the lock off the door because he was out here earlier and forgot to latch it. "You want to piss away your profits?" I say, my voice ringing out in the still morning air. "It's all the same to me. Just let me know before everything's gone so I can still get out when the getting's good."

That makes me stop, makes *him* stop, and my hands tremble as the impact of what I've said hits me full force. *So I can still get out...*is that where we're heading? Me leaving him? Is this all because of Luke? "Kent," I start, turning. My lover stares at me incredulously, did I just say I would leave him? Behind him I see Luke on the other side of the screen door, watching us. Did I honestly *admit...* "Oh shit," I murmur. Now it's me reaching for him, it's my touch that's shrugged away. "Kent, I didn't mean it like that."

"Like what?" he wants to know. Beneath the brim of his hat, his eyes are dark and unreadable—whatever emotions whirl through him right now, whatever he's thinking, he's keeping it to himself, I'm not privy to it. "Don't let me keep you here, kid. If the money's not good for you, don't let *me* stop you from leaving."

I ball my hands into useless fists and lean my head back to stare at the cloudless sky. "It's not the money," I tell him, frustrated. Can't he *see* that? His little business makes enough to pay the bills and keep us fed, that's about it. "This has *nothing* to do with your money, Kent. I don't ask for any, do I? I don't *want* any." When I look at him, I see the hard set of his jaw and know that he doesn't believe me. Lowering my voice so Luke won't overhear, I say, "It's your drinking."

"Spending my *money* on drinks," he clarifies.

He doesn't *get* it. "No!" I cry. "It's nipping at the bottle when you get up first thing, Kent. It's finishing a six-pack by noon. It's being too goddamn *drunk* by end of the day to want to fool around, *that's* what this is about. I'm sick and tired of being pushed aside for everything else in your life."

Taking a step closer to me, Kent pokes at my chest with one finger, a sharp touch that I swear bruises, the hurt lingers long after I brush his hand away. "Whether you've noticed or not, I'm trying to run a business here," he snarls. "I work hard, every *day* slaving out in that market just so we can make it. I don't ask for much from you, Marcus. I don't make you pay for your meals or your room, do I?" I try to turn from him but he grips my shoulder, forces me to look into his angry face. "So I like a drink or two now and then to unwind. Lay off me about it, you hear?"

I twist out of his hands. "Fine," I mutter. *Get yourself killed,* I think, heading for the barn. *Drink yourself to death, fine, see if I care.* I don't, I tell myself, I *don't.* I kick open the wooden door, feel the dry stench of hay rise up at me from inside the barn, and tears blur my vision, I have to wipe them away with the back of my hand. If I don't care then why the *fuck* am I crying over this?

✳

HE'S GOING TO COME in after me, I just know it. I sit on the bales of hay and wait, the dark barn hot around me despite the early hour. He'll come in and talk to me, tell me I'm wrong, tell me he loves me—does he love me? He's never said the words out loud. I can't even imagine what they'd sound like in his voice.

Time passes—I'm not sure how much, how long it is I sit there in the heat and the hay, waiting. At some point I lie down, stretch out on the itchy straw, stare up at the warped boards that form the roof and squint at the sky beyond. He's not coming in here. He doesn't care, either. Fuck him.

Sometime later, I realize I'm not angry anymore. Tired, yes. Weary… God, so damn weary. But in the center of my chest where my anger roiled is nothing, just a deep, empty ache, and that scares me. What happened to the way we were? What happened to the easy relationship we shared, the camaraderie, the sex?

Luke.

He happened, came into our lives and shook us up, shook *me* up, made me see what I've been too blind to admit to myself all this time, made me see what it is I want and God help me, it's not Kent. It's Luke, I want him more than I'm willing to admit. He makes me feel like I haven't felt in years—desirable and young and free, virginal again, everything about him is heady and exciting and new. How can I not want someone like him in my life?

I'm just mad. What the hell am I thinking? So we get in a fight once, I'm ready to walk out? What does that say about *me?*

I don't know. And right now I don't care to know, I'm not going to think about it anymore. I've had it with thinking, my head hurts and the more I sit here stewing, the less I'm getting done. So I slide off the bale I'm on and look around the barn, hands on my hips. I'll clean this up, it's not that bad—I could be out in the fields picking ripened vegetables, that would be hot work in this sun, but at least here it's shady and a little cool, and there's not really a lot to do. The hay in the stall needs to be pitched, the bales scattered around need to be stacked, that's about it. A few hours of mindless labor and I'll get whatever mood's eating at me out of my system, I'll work past this indecision tearing me apart, I'll be able to move on. I won't think of anything until I'm finished in here, not Luke, not Kent, *nothing*. It'll be a relief really. Nothing at all.

Only it doesn't quite work out that way. I concentrate on the bales of hay and get them stacked up against the side of the horse stall by the way the sun's traveled across the roof. I guess it's still early, just after noon, no later than two at the most. I'm making good time, I'll finish up in here in another hour or so and then head inside, shower, take a nap…*dream of Luke,* I think, but I shake that away, I'm not entertaining those thoughts right now, am I?

But Pandora's box has been opened and images rise unbidden in my mind. Luke in my bed, twirling that daisy between his fingers, listening to me and Kent in the shower. Last night on the couch, the two of us pressed together, his genitals so soft against mine, his kisses the very breath of heaven itself. And when I turn towards the stall to start on the hay there, I see him again, stretched out on the tamped straw, that hat covering his face while he pretended to sleep.

I play out the scene in my mind, me peering in at him with the thrill of discovery coursing through my body, only this time he's naked, the hat the only thing he wears, and his dick lies along the curve of his thigh, his ass begs to be entered, his skin is a burnished gold in the shadows. I see myself kneeling beside him, my fingers tracing along his belly, his balls, he moans beneath me and rolls onto his back, exposing himself to me fully. I ease his legs apart, kneel between them, lean down until the scent of his musk fills my nose and stirs my groin, and when I lick up his thick length, already hard, his hand grasps the hat that hides his face to stifle his low cry.

I can *hear* how he'd sound, it makes me weak and I fall to my knees on the hay where he slept a few nights back. Before I can stop myself or even think about what I'm doing, I unzip my jeans, push them down my thighs, pull down my boxers and I'm already hard myself, my dick stands out from the patch of hair at my crotch like a steel rod, throbbing for release. It won't take long—kneeling in the hay, my pants down, my ass exposed, one hand on my erection and squeezing my balls, rubbing below to the tender skin that Luke called the taint, the other hand cupping my ass, parting my cheeks, rimming until I gasp out his name, I push into myself and want to sob, I need him so bad, I *want* him and not just my hand on my ass and cock, I want *him*—

The door creaks faintly as someone steps into the barn.

Cowboy 73

I freeze, one finger in myself, my dick already weeping, I'm so close to coming, I have to bite my lower lip to keep from whimpering in desire. I hear footsteps and want to call out, *who's there?* Kent, and he'd see me here masturbating, he'd probably tell me I could've asked and just push my hands away, enter me and thrust a few times before growing bored. Or Luke, what would he say if he caught me? Would he want to watch? Join me? Take matters into his own hands?

I imagine his strong hands moving mine aside, one finger slipping deep into me, others encircling me, kneading, working me hard...I'd rock back into his hand, pull him as far inside as he could get, I'd fuck his hand and scream out his name when I got off. What if it's *him?*

It is. His voice echoes through the rafters when he calls out softly, "Marcus? You still in here?"

Suddenly embarrassed, I pull out of myself, wipe my hand on the hay as I stand, shove myself back into my jeans and haul them up. My boxers catch in the zipper and for a few tense moments I can't get them free, I'm struggling here, I swear my crotch is growing damp and he'll come around the bales of hay and see me here, he'll want to know what I'm doing, he'll want to know why my pants are undone— "Marcus?"

The zipper slides up with a sigh, *thank you, Jesus.* "Here," I call out, my voice shaky and uneven. I run a hand through my hair to push it out of my eyes and busy myself with the hay, I'm supposed to be cleaning up, not making more of a mess. When Luke steps into view, he leans against the bales I've stacked and shoves his hands into the pockets of his jeans, grins at me. His shirt hangs open to reveal his bare chest, the muscles glistening with sweat that I want to lick away. "Hey Luke."

"Hey Marcus." His cowboy hat rides low over his brow, but he tips it back and winks at me. "Come here."

I shouldn't, I'm with Kent, I shouldn't fool around with him but the look he gives me does me in, despite whatever resolve I think I might have, I'm weak against it. My fingers tremble as I reach for him—he lets me touch his flat stomach, his hard chest, and the brim of his hat fits easily on the top of my head when we kiss. I feel like he knows what I was doing, he tastes it on my lips, feels it when his hand trails down my body to toy with the zipper of my jeans. "Missed you," he sighs. How long has it been? Just a few hours. Kent was gone almost a full day and never said that to me.

"What's he have you doing?" I ask, taking a step back. I want to widen the distance between us because when I stand so close to him, I don't trust myself.

But my hand stays on the waistband of his jeans, *my* jeans, and my fingers ease behind the buckle of his belt to press along fluttering skin. "Grass seed," Luke tells me with a laugh, and he catches my wrist before I can move too far away. "I've got to reseed the plot behind the sunflowers. Come here, Marcus, he's not around."

He reels me in like a prized catch, drapes one arm around my neck to keep me close. Tentatively I rest my head on his shoulder, thread an arm around his waist, Kent's not here. Luke kisses my forehead and when he speaks, his words tickle my skin. "I was hoping you hadn't thrown out this hay yet. I'm gonna need it to cover the seed." His lips press against my cheekbone, my upper lip, and he breathes, "That's my story, if he wants to know why I'm in here with you."

I let out a thin giggle that he cuts off with a kiss, this one deeper than the others, insistent, it presses me back against the beam that makes up one corner of the horse stall and I stagger beneath the need I feel in him, my hands clench into fists in his shirt. "What happened this morning?" he asks, kissing me before I can answer. "Was it about me?"

"I don't know," I admit, my words lost in his lips. His mouth moves lower, around the curve of my jaw, down my throat, sucking at me as I lean back and gasp his name. "Luke—"

"Did he ask if we fool around?" he persists. I shake my head—as far as I know, Kent doesn't even suspect us of anything. "Did he say something about me staying here?"

"No, nothing like that." I cradle his face in my hands, raise him to me for another kiss. "He got a little pissed about the flower but he thinks I picked it. He likes you."

With a coy grin, Luke kisses me again. I feel the curve of his smile against my lips, taste his breath as he murmurs, "The way you do?"

That makes me laugh. My reply is another kiss, but it's not enough for Luke, he presses his body against mine, pins me to the beam, his hips grinding into mine. "How do you like me, Marcus?" he wants to know. "I see it in your eyes when you look at me, I feel it when we touch but I want to hear you say it."

I love you, I think, but when I open my mouth, the words don't come. I've never said them to Kent, it's been years since I've heard them in my voice, I can't just blurt them out to this runaway boy. As we kiss, he stares at me, my own eyes flutter open to meet his violet gaze and then I have to close them again, I can't watch him while we make out, not if he reads the words in my eyes. *I love you.* They burn in me, a fire that sets my body aflame.

I love you.

He shrugs out of his shirt, lies it down on the hay where he slept. "Sit here," he tells me, patting the shirt. Before I can comply, he unzips my jeans and I let him push them down to the floor. "Damn, Marcus," he laughs, seeing my still-hard erection poke at the front of my boxers. "My kisses do this to you?"

A thin blush creeps into my cheeks, heating my face. "I was sort of already…" I trail off, embarrassed. "Kind of in the middle of…when you came in…"

Luke nudges me and winks. "Good thing I stopped by," he jokes, and then my boxers are gone, around my ankles with my jeans. "Down, boy."

I sit on his shirt, the hay crunching beneath my ass, my legs spread in an undignified pose. Luke doesn't seem to care, though—he kneels between my knees, rubs a hand along my stomach. "Lie back," he says, and when I comply, propped up on my elbows, he nods encouragingly. "Like that, good." His hands stroke my inner thighs, massaging them, making my cock stiffen again, how's he do that? Without even touching me *there*, he has me aching and ready all over again. "You're beautiful, Marcus, has he ever told you that?"

I lean back, let my head loll between my shoulders, moan softly in reply. No, Kent's never told me that. I'm good, I've got a great ass, I'm tight, but beautiful? It's up there with love, another word I'll never hear him say.

Those hands, they knead my thighs, parting my legs until the shirt is clenched between my buttocks. Those fingers caress my throbbing flesh, tracing circles around my balls, rubbing the skin at the base of my shaft. I thrust up into the slight touch, wanting more, needing more, and I'm just about to beg for him to do whatever it is he has in mind and get it over with, I'm *dying* here, when I feel a drop of hot saliva course down my length. Through half-closed eyes I see him hovering above my erection, mouth open, salivating for me, and he waits until he knows I'm looking before he goes down.

His lips are like velvet, soft and firm. His cheeks suck at me, his tongue swirls down my cock, licks my balls, twirls back up to run circles around the tip. Down again, all the way in, I thrust into him so hard that I rise up off the hay and his hands cup my ass, his fingers part my cheeks, rub me until I cry out, I want him in me. I clench my fists into the hay as he sucks at me, saliva dripping down my balls and cooling on my fevered skin, he takes me in completely and hums until I'm close to tears, I need release, I need *him*.

Then he pulls up, his lips leaving a wet trail that ends at the tip of my dick, he sucks on the spongy head and hums again and *God* but it's mind-numbing, for once everything is completely blank, all I know is this sensation, these hands, this tongue, nothing else exists, nothing even comes *close*.

His tongue licks below my balls, rims around his own fingers that press into me, I arch into his hands and mouth and sob his name. I rake my hands through the hay as I rise to meet him, each thrust of mine met with his wet lips, his hot mouth. He takes me in again, his fingers in me, me in him, and I can't help it, I want it, I want *him* and I buck beneath him, scream his name to the rafters, my voice startling the bats that roost there. For the first time in forever, I hold nothing back, and when I come, it's in an explosive rush that leaves me as weak as a newborn kitten, mewling his name.

He drinks me down, every last drop, then sucks until I'm half-hard again, finger-fucks me until I start to thrust back. I'm ready for more. But he slips out of me, lets me go, smoothes a hand across my stomach as he crawls on top of me and presses me back against the hay. His kisses are sweet with my cum, I taste myself in every corner of his mouth, and I feel his own erection bite into me through his jeans. "Tell me, Marcus," he murmurs between kisses, and I nod—right now, the state I'm in, what he's reduced me to? I'll tell him anything. His lips form the words against my mouth. "Does he do that to you? Can he make you feel like *this*?"

"No." The word is lost in our kisses, but it's there, it's audible, it flashes in my mind like a neon sign and if I didn't realize it before, I know it now—in this instant, whatever I had or thought I had with Kent is over.

There's only Luke.

part 3

I help Luke load the loose hay into a wheelbarrow, then he takes the handles and, with a smile, tells me, "Get in." And because it's silly and childish, because I'm still high from him, because I know Kent will get pissed if he finds us goofing off like this, I clamber on top of the hay, pull my legs up under me so they don't dangle, grip the sides of the wheelbarrow and lean back to look up at Luke. He grins down, kisses the tip of my nose, wiggles the unsteady cart in his hands and says, "Hold on, sexy." *Sexy,* I like that. It rekindles the fire that smolders deep inside of me, fans the flames of my lust, makes me burn for Luke. If Kent only knew what a word like that does to me, he'd never use my name.

I hold on tight as Luke races through the fields, the ride bumpy over gravel and uneven grass, and by the time we reach the plot behind the sunflowers, we're both giggling like little kids. Skidding to a stop, Luke skirts the wheelbarrow and plops into my lap, his arms around my neck, his naked chest and dusty jeans hot against my hands, his lips on mine. "Marcus," he sighs as he climbs onto me, trying to find a comfortable position, his hands fisting in my collar, my hair, my hands on his denim-clad ass and easing between his legs. Right here, in the middle of the damn field, far enough from the road to avoid being seen but what if Kent decides to come check up on Luke for some reason? What if he catches us out here in the open?

Something shifts beneath me and without warning, the wheelbarrow lurches to one side. I hear a thin *snap,* one of the wooden legs breaking away beneath our combined weight, and then we're dumped unceremoniously to the ground, a jumble of arms and legs and hay. Luke's beneath me, the blue grass seed like a lint-flecked blanket under his tanned shoulders, and his eyes sparkle wide with mirth. "Oh shit," he laughs, toying with the collar of my shirt. "*You* broke it."

"*You* broke it," I giggle. When I try to sit up, though, he pulls me to him for a hungry kiss. "He's going to be pissed," I whisper.

Luke picks hay from my hair and murmurs, "You said we don't talk about him when it's just us, remember?"

"Him who?" I ask playfully. Luke kisses me again, his knee rising between my legs to press at another erection already coming up.

Here in the heat of the sun, it's hard to pull myself away from the boy, he's more intoxicating than all of Kent's bottled spirits combined. But I know my lover, all too well—after two years of living with the man, I know the anger from this morning has simmered in him all day and sooner or later he's going to come looking for someone to take it out on. Probably me, he'll head for the barn because it's closer than the fields and he'll want to know why I'm still not finished sweeping out that damn horse stall, he'll wonder why I'm not there when I'm supposed to be. And he may be drunk as a fish already but he's not stupid. He'll know I'm with Luke, even if he doesn't suspect what it is we're doing, and then he'll come out *here* to get me and I don't want that. I don't want him ruining this.

Still, it takes everything I have to pull away from Luke, and his eager lips, his insistent hands. Together we splint the wheelbarrow's leg—not broken, thank God, but badly cracked, I'm already thinking maybe I'll tell Kent I caught it in a rut going too fast and it just snapped, he's already mad at me anyway. "You go on back, Marcus," Luke tells me as he starts to spread the hay over the seed. "This won't take long. Maybe you can glue that and he won't have to know—"

"He'll know," I say, frowning at the wheelbarrow. "He's not blind, Luke."

With a laugh, he winks at me over his shoulder and jokes, "Could've fooled me." Before I can ask what he means by that, he takes my hand and tugs gently. I step closer and lean down for an offered kiss. "He can't see you, Marcus," he whispers, his words warm against my cheek, and I have to close my eyes to keep back sudden tears. *Can't see me...* "He's blind if he can't see how much you need to be loved, Marcus, and if he *can* see that, if he *knows,* then he's a goddamn fool not to love you like you deserve."

"Luke," I sigh, my throat tight with emotion. I don't want to hear this.

His hand tightens on mine and his lips brush my mouth in a soft kiss. "All my life I've searched people's faces, Marcus, looking for something I could never find. Love, maybe, acceptance, lust, I don't know. Something more than a drunk's hate and anger staring back." I look into his shimmering eyes and can't imagine anyone hating this boy, not when my whole body trills with the thought of loving him. "I know you must love some part of Kent, and I'm cool with that. I'm not asking you to give him up, that's your call. But don't turn me away, please." His lower lip trembles, I feel it against my chin, and I squat down to envelop him in a tight embrace. "I like the way you look at me," he breathes. "Don't close your eyes. I've been looking for something like you for so long, I'm not going to lose it now."

Rubbing my hands across his back, I promise him, "You won't."

I know how he feels, I've done the same thing myself, searched forever for something I was almost sure I'd never find. Until now. *He's* what I see when I look at Kent, *he's* what I want when I think of the boys in my magazine ads, the cowboy I had begun to believe no longer existed. But it does exist, it's him, *him,* and I'm not letting that slip away.

✻

IT DOESN'T TAKE LONG to sweep out the horse stall, but with each move I can feel bits of straw working down the back of my shirt and beneath my sleeves until I'm itchy and raw from scratching at myself through the thin material. I need a shower and something to eat, it's almost dinnertime, and probably a nap wouldn't hurt either. I'm not used to this physical labor, sitting under the tent by the register day in and day out. I wonder what business was like today, how many plants and vegetables Kent sold, how much profit he kept and how much he'll give me at the end of the day.

If he gives it to me—I have a feeling that remark I made this morning, about getting out when the getting's good, I think that might have shaken him up more than he'll care to admit. I know it scared the hell out of *me*.

With the barn out of the way, I retreat to the cool house, unzipping my jeans before I'm even through the screen door, shucking them down in the hall, tearing my shirt off over my head and stepping out of my boots, my pants, my boxers. By the time I reach the bathroom I'm naked, my clothes strewn out behind me like shed skin, and I don't even pull the shower curtain closed before I turn the water on. The spray is hot and hard against my tired skin, like solid sunlight hitting my back and shoulders and ass, and I stand beneath the downpour, let the water trickle down my face, over my closed eyes, into my partly open mouth. It tastes clean like Luke, and I remember his words, *don't close your eyes, don't turn me away.* How could he think I'd be able to do that? After the few stolen moments we've had together, how could he possibly think I wouldn't want for more?

And what the fuck am I going to tell Kent?

I love him, but somehow I don't think that'll be enough, because Luke is right, part of me still loves Kent too, or whatever it is I see when I look at him. I love who I think he could be, and that's not something I'm ready to throw away just yet. He's given me two years here in his house, he's been good to me. The drinking I've learned to live with, it's not like he gets mean or violent, he's never hit me. He just...how did Luke put it? He just doesn't see me, he can't, he *won't*, and somehow that neglect is worse than any abuse I might have suffered at his hands. How many nights did I lie alone in my bed and pray for him to come to me? How many days did I sit in the heat of that tent and long for a touch, a wink, a *smile*? Would that have been so hard?

He's not affectionate, a voice inside me whispers.

No, he's not, I know this. My first night here, I was the one who made the move, after I grilled steaks on the barbeque out back. It was me who looked at him from across the picnic table, me who smiled slowly, me who reached out to cover his hand, and he was already half lit, of course he responded to my advance, how could he not? I knew he'd been drinking, that made it so easy, just a few soft words and my thumb along the back of his wrist, and we didn't even make it into the house. We did it right there on the table, paper plates pushed aside and the evening sun shining low on the horizon as I stood with my legs spread, my jeans around my ankles, my upper body lying over the polished redwood. He's always been a quick lover, a selfish man, but that first time, outside? After the way those women gawked over him all day?

As he thrust into me then, I thought this was it, this man, this *cowboy,* he was mine and that was all I wanted, all I came west to find. He pulled out of me as he came, hot juices trickling down my ass and thighs, and I came just at the *thought* of him, the image I had in my mind of the two of us together, him behind me and me bent over the picnic table, his strong hands on my hips, his cowboy hat cocked back at a roguish angle.

What happened to that image? That man?

It's my fault, really, this whole thing. I know it, I feel guilt wash over me like the shower spray. The drinking he did before we met but I could've been a better lover, I could've loved him more and made the alcohol unnecessary. He shouldn't need it in his life, not if he has me, not if I were *enough*

...and this whole thing with Luke, my fault again, I'm the one unsatisfied, I'm the one with the folder full of jerk-off boys beneath my bed, I'm the one who turned to another man to find what I should've been looking for in Kent all along. He deserves someone better than me, someone stronger. He works hard every single day, gives me shelter and food and sex, how horrible am I to turn my back on that for a boy with a sweet smile and pretty eyes? What more am I looking for, what more could I possibly need?

Love.

Kent loves me, he *has* to. But he doesn't say it and I'm not a fucking mind reader, I don't just *know* these things. That night he spent in jail, did he worry about me? Did he hope I was alright, did he care? When he's in town or in his market with his plants, does he think about me? Does his mind drift away to my touch, my voice, my smile?

If it did, would I still find Luke so irresistibly appealing?

❈

OUT OF THE SHOWER, dressed, my clothes scooped up from the floor and shoved into the washer, I rummage through the kitchen looking for something to cook for dinner. This is my job, this is what I do in exchange for the food, the room, the job behind the register. I cook, and I keep the house clean, and I do the laundry, women's work but Kent doesn't do it, he had a girl who used to come in twice a week before I showed up. What's going to happen when I tell him about Luke? *Am* I going to tell him?

I have to. I have to.

But he's not here, it's just me in the house right now, I won't think about it. I find noodles in the cabinet, a jar of tomato sauce behind a bottle of Jim Beam—spaghetti tonight. What will Kent do if I'm not here to cook for him? To keep track of his expenses, his profits? *He survived for years before you came along,* I tell myself. *He'll manage when you're gone.*

Has it come down to this? Am I leaving him?

I can't imagine anything else. I love Luke, I do, I want that boy so bad, just *thinking* of him stirs my groin. I want his kisses and his hands on me and his laugh, his smile, his eyes shining at me. At the sink, I look out the kitchen window to the market down by the road, and from here I can see Kent moving through the customers, his bare skin glistening with sweat, his jeans riding low, that hat...Luke's right, I love him, too, or a part of him that I'm not willing to give up. How the hell have I managed to do this to myself? What the fuck do I do now?

Nothing, not yet. Not until I have to.

Okay, *that* I can do, nothing at all, I'll keep the way I feel for Luke a secret from Kent, he doesn't *have* to know, at least not yet. Not until I figure out what I'm going to do, what *we're* going to do, Luke and I, we're in this together. So what do I tell Kent?

Nothing.

Somehow, it's not much of a comfort, but it keeps the fear at bay, it dulls the gnawing anxiety that eats away at my heart and makes my hands shake. I can do nothing, I've done it before. Hell, the last two years have been just that, me turning a blind eye to Kent's drinking, my unhappiness, and Luke is only a long overdue wake-up call.

I push both men from my thoughts and concentrate on making dinner. If I'm not going to do anything right this second, I'm not going to drive myself crazy worrying about what *will* happen when I finally tell Kent, I don't have any control over that. So for now I'll focus on getting through dinner to a time when my lover falls asleep and Luke is mine again. I've been doing it for the past few days, this routine is one I'm getting good at. I can do this, I know I can.

I have to.

✻

DINNER IS EATEN IN silence, as usual, tensions between the three of us strained because I was right, Kent's still holding a grudge against me for my harsh words this morning. He wants an apology that he's simply not going to get.

After he's finished eating, he stands and digs into his pocket, pulls out a wad of dollar bills, a handful of change that he scatters on the table in front of me. "That's it?" I ask, skeptical. Roughly a hundred dollars, maybe a little more—I wonder how many twenties are folded into his back pocket, hidden in the space where his flask curves away from his ass.

"It's been slow," Kent tells me, the scowl on his face daring me to contradict him. I close my hand over the rolled bills and keep my mouth shut. He sits down again, picks at the noodles on his plate with his fork, and asks, "Did you get the barn done?"

"Yeah." I don't expect any gratitude, but it still hurts when he doesn't even say *thank you*. How hard would that be?

Instead, he takes another mouthful of spaghetti and nods, yes, that's good, it's done. Then he glances at Luke, who tells him without prompting, "Got the seed down like you asked. Marcus helped me cover it with the hay—"

Now Kent glares at me. "You busted a bale for that?" he asks.

"I used what was in the stall, babe," I say, stumbling over the word. Kent frowns into his plate—how much has he had to drink today?—and I think that this might not be a good time to mention the broken wheelbarrow. Across from me, Luke raises an eyebrow but stays quiet. Softly, I tell Kent, "I didn't open another bale, just used what was already out, is all." When he doesn't answer—I don't expect him to—I curl my hand into a fist around the money on the table and murmur, "Thanks for the deposit."

"Told you I'd give it to you," he grumbles. Then he pushes the plate away and stands a second time, shoves his chair in, opens the fridge for a can of beer, and I think that's it, that's all he's going to say, when he adds, "Don't fight with me, Marcus. I'm about tired of it."

I have to swallow back my anger, *don't fight with me.* As if the whole episode this morning was *my* fault. As if he's the only one who worked up a sweat today, the only one tired now, the only one who doesn't want another argument. *Fuck you,* I think, biting my lower lip to keep the words inside, where he can't hear them and they won't get me into trouble. *What's keeping me here with you?* I wonder as I glare at his broad back. He doesn't look at me, just disappears into the living room and doesn't even look over his shoulder. *What's keeping me from taking off with Luke tonight and leaving you to drink yourself to death?*

Nothing. Not a damn thing.

Across from me, Luke gives me a halfhearted smile and whispers, "It's okay, Marcus."

"I didn't..." My words trail off in a sad sigh, I don't know what I want to say. It doesn't matter anyway, does it? I twist my fork through my noodles but I'm finished eating. I don't want any more.

Beneath the table Luke's foot comes up between my legs, his toes curling into my crotch gently. "I know," he says. "It's okay, I know."

※

I WASH THE DISHES and hand them to Luke—even though we have a drainer, he insists on drying each plate. "It's an excuse to stand close to you," he says, his voice low so it won't carry out into the living room, where Kent's watching TV. He has it up so damn loud, I'd be surprised if he *could* hear anything else. The more he drinks, I swear the louder it gets.

And Luke is practically standing on top of me, he's so close. When I scrub a plate, my elbow pokes into his side, and every so often he'll bump my hip with his to make me smile. At one point, I'm scouring the pot and he's leaning over the sink, waiting for me to finish so he can towel it off, and his arm snakes around my waist, his hand eases into my front pocket, his fingers slip beneath the money I've shoved in there to squeeze at my crotch. "You're stacked, baby," he tells me, but I'm not sure if he means the money or my dick, already hardening beneath his touch.

I turn away and his hand falls from my pocket. "Kent," I warn—the last thing I need is to have him amble into the kitchen for another beer and find us cuddling.

"We could leave now," Luke says. I look at him sharply, only to find those violet eyes staring back, serene. Is he serious? Just walk out now and never look back? I couldn't do that to Kent. With a nod at my pocket, Luke adds, "You've got some money. How far do you think that'd get us?"

I hand him the pot, a little too roughly. "It's Kent's money," I remind him. I'm not quite sure how to take him—his quick smile tells me he's joking but the eager gleam in his eyes, that suggests something more. "Not mine."

Luke drops his gaze to the pot as he dries it, a slight pout on his lips. "I've got some," he mumbles.

Turning on the spigot, I rinse my hands and try to figure out just what it is he's saying. "You want to leave?" I ask, frowning at him. When he shrugs, I want to know, "Where'd you get money from?" I hate the suspicious part of me that feels like checking the deposit but I know he hasn't been in it, I keep the bank bags in Kent's closet, Luke hasn't been in *there*. He doesn't answer immediately, and I prompt, "Luke? What's this all about?"

With another shrug, he tells me, "Maybe nothing. I'm just..." He rubs at the pot in his hands, doesn't look at me. "I just don't like seeing you like this," he says, speaking softly. I have to turn off the water to hear his words as he explains, "All bent out of shape because he's being a bastard. I was just talking shit, Marcus, saying maybe we could run away together. You know, like dreaming out loud? Just talking shit, that's all."

Dreaming out loud, I like that. I give him a shy smile and now it's my hip that nudges his, causing him to finally look up at me. "And you'd use Kent's money," I joke. "Somehow I don't think it'd get us very far. He kept most of it himself."

Luke's pout dissolves into his sunny grin, and his eyes light up. Setting the pot into the drainer with the rest of the clean dishes, he reminds me, "I've got a little cash."

"From where?" I ask again. I seem to remember him telling me about stashing a wallet in our barn, that first night he stayed in the house, when it was just me and him and Kent wasn't around to curb our talk or keep our voices low. "How much are you talking, Luke?"

Wringing out the towel, he lowers his voice until I can barely hear him speak. "Couple hundred," he says, and my mind whirls out in a million directions all at once. A couple *hundred*? Where's a boy like this get money like that? He must see the incredulous look on my face because he hastens to add, "It's not what you're thinking. Well, it sort of is, but not like that."

I'm thinking— "You stole it," I whisper.

From the way he can't meet my gaze, I know I'm right. "I didn't *rob* anyone," he assures me. "Like hold up a store or something, I'm not that bad. It's my dad's, okay? I took it before I left. He has this cookie jar full of dollars in the kitchen behind the stove, I know he didn't think I knew about it, but I'd seen it once after school and I counted it when he wasn't home, just to see how much he had." He looks at me, fear written in his eyes, he's scared I'm going to hate him now, he thinks I'll turn him away. *Don't,* I can read the plea in his purple gaze, *please don't*. "Believe me, Marcus, I only took a little bit. Just a few big bills from the bottom of the jar, that's it. If he even knew how much he's saved up in there, he'd never miss it, I promise."

I don't know what to say. I find myself thinking to the deposit bags in Kent's closet, I wonder if Luke knows about *them*. Tentatively, he touches the bulge of bills in my pocket, looks at me with beseeching eyes, and whispers, "I was just teasing about this, Marcus, believe me. I wouldn't take Kent's money. He's been nothing but good to me, and I know how you feel for him. I was just kidding about running away. Really."

Taking a deep breath to steady my racing heart, I say, "I'm not running out on him, Luke." He nods quickly, yes, he knows, and this time when his fingers ease into my pocket, I don't brush them away. "I'm going to tell him about…about us," I say, and Luke nods at that, too. "I just—I don't know when or how, and it probably won't be pretty, but I have to tell him myself. You see that, don't you? I owe him that much, at least."

A gentle tug on my pocket brings me a step closer to Luke, who closes his eyes and presses his lips to mine in a brief kiss. "I know," he murmurs, his words mere breath against my skin. I squeeze my eyes shut as his hands find my waist and he kisses me a second time. "I'm cool with whatever you decide," he says. "If you want to go, I'm leaving with you. If you stay, I want to stay, too. You're what I've been looking for my whole life, Marcus. I'm going to do whatever I must to keep up with you."

And why doesn't Kent ever say such lovely things?

From the other room he calls out my name. I push against Luke and he calls out again. "Kent," I whisper, turning away. For good measure I take a step back and when Luke leans against me, I put a hand on his chest to keep some distance between us. Staring into his eyes, I raise my voice and reply, "Yeah, hon?"

Luke sniggers at that, *hon*. I poke at his stomach to keep him quiet, and he rests his head on my shoulder. "Kent? What do you want? I'm sort of doing the dishes here…"

Which I'm not, we're finished, but he doesn't need to know that. Luke's breath tickles along my neck, beneath my collar, and I wonder how much longer Kent's going to be up. Hasn't he had enough to drink yet? Can't he head off to bed and leave us alone already?

Apparently that's asking too much. "Another beer," he grumbles, and I sigh as I push at Luke. Another beer. Like he hasn't had his fill yet. Like he can't get up off his drunk ass and come in here to get one.

"I've got it," Luke murmurs before I can object. As he ducks into the fridge, he asks, "Maybe we can go for a walk or something? If you want."

Good idea. "Sure," I say. I lean back against the sink and watch him, he moves so gracefully, all thin lines and flat planes, I remember the barn this morning and want him above me again, his arms around me, his hands on me, his tongue and lips in delicious parts of my body. At the doorway between the rooms he turns to wink at me, and that makes me grin. What did I ever do to find someone like him, after all this time? And what am I going to do keep him?

And what am I going to do about Kent?

✶

LUKE SLIPS OUT THE back door and waits for me to follow. "We'll be outside," I tell Kent, passing between him and the TV so he has to see me. Even though I already know the answer, I ask anyway, "Do you want to come for a walk?"

"I'm watching TV," he replies, in that slow, *are you stupid?* tone of voice he has that he uses with me when he's drunk. When I start to say something else, tell him be back soon, he raises one hand and glares at the television, he doesn't want to hear it. *Fine,* I think, pulling the screen door shut behind me.

Luke's hand eases into mine and he kisses my cheek, a small peck that Kent doesn't see because he's glued to the set. "Come on," he whispers, pulling me along after him into the night. His hand is warm in my own, his fingers strong and sure, and with each step we take, he swings our hands in the space between us. "Where do you want to go?"

I shrug—there's really nowhere *to* go. I'd suggest the barn again but what if Kent comes out looking for us? Another hour or two and he'll fall asleep, and I can curl up beside Luke on the couch again, we'll kiss and cuddle and make love the way we did yesterday, no intercourse but God, somehow so much more.

So we just hold hands, and Luke leads me around the side of the house to the front. On the porch I ignore the wicker chairs and glass-top table we have set up to look out over the market. Instead, I sit down with my back against the railing, my legs stretched out towards the kitchen door—from here I can see the doorway that leads into the living room, and the footrest of Kent's recliner, the bottoms of his bare feet. "Sit down," I say softly, tugging at Luke's hand. He sinks to the porch beside me, his hip and leg pressed against mine. "Can you see him?" he asks, leaning in front of me to glance through the screen door.

I push him back playfully. "I see him," I say as I ease an arm between Luke's waist and the railing. Watching Kent's feet, I pull Luke a little closer, until his head drops to my shoulder, and he touches my chin to make me look at him. Here in the dusk, the light that falls through the kitchen window and screen door illuminates his face and deepens his eyes until they're the color of inky pools, I could drown in their depths and never resurface. I love him, I know it utterly and completely, I've fallen for him harder in these past few days than I ever fell for Kent in the two years I've known him. And I need to tell him that. I need to let him go.

Luke's lips touch mine, a tender kiss that I pull away from despite the lust roiling through my veins. "I have to keep an eye on him," I murmur—this close, our noses touching, our temples together, there's no need to talk above a whisper. I sure as hell don't want Kent stumbling into the kitchen for another beer only to see us on the porch making out. My hand on Luke's hip tickles beneath his shirt, along his flat stomach, and I give him another kiss before leaning back against the railing. The porch floor is hard beneath my ass, almost uncomfortable, but Luke is soft in my embrace, warm against me, and the night is young. *Soon,* I think, rubbing his side as I stare into the living room, vigilant.

Luke buries his face in my neck, his breath hot along my hair, his lips damp and warm on my skin. His tongue licks out, tastes the flesh below my ear. His fingers find the top button of my shirt, the next, and the next, until my shirt's parted enough for his hand to slip inside. He thumbs over my nipple, already hard from the breath in my ear, the lips sucking at me, the body against mine, and then his hand smoothes over my ribs, under my arm, around my back as he half-climbs onto me.

I wonder how stoic my face looks as I sit here in the midst of these caresses. In the living room, Kent's recliner hasn't moved—his pale feet form a V above the foot-rest and the sounds from the TV drift out to where we sit, my body slowly responding to Luke's lips, his hands, his tongue.

Nosing the collar of my shirt aside, he kisses the curve of my throat, the shelf of my collarbone. Almost without realizing it, my hand finds the cleft between his legs, my fingers know their way around without my having to look away from the open door and Kent beyond.

When I unzip his jeans, unsnap his boxers, take his solid length in my hand and start to knead gently, Luke's moans fill the night. So loud, drowning out the rest of the world, the TV, the cars that pass down the road, and I giggle as he thrusts into me, practically crawling on top of me in his need. But Kent doesn't hear him—these breathless gasps, these soft groans, my name whispered in a heated rush, they eclipse my world but don't stray far from the porch. His lips are pressed against my ear, his hands strum my chest, his dick hardens in my hand with each squeeze, each thrust.

Maybe we won't have to wait until Kent goes to bed to get together. Maybe I can help Luke find release here, and just thinking of his juices in my hand makes my jeans chafe my own erection. I imagine him fucking into my fingers until he comes, thick white cum that'll slick my hand and wrist, and I'll lick them clean while he watches me with hooded eyes, I'll touch the tip of his nose with one wet finger and lick the dampness off that I leave behind. I haven't tasted another boy in forever, sure as hell not *Kent* and his thin cum that's more beer than anything else. I wonder if Luke tastes like I imagine he does, sweet and maybe slightly salty, just a little bit bitter and completely insatiable—

In the living room, Kent pushes the footrest of the recliner down.

He stands, wavers unsteadily on his feet, then clicks off the TV. "Oh shit," I mutter, letting Luke slip from my fingers even as he thrusts into my palm. I tug my shirt closed, fumble with the buttons, watch as my lover crosses the living room, heading for the kitchen. "He's up."

"Up," Luke murmurs, not quite comprehending the word. I glance at him and see eyes dull with lust, lips swollen, and I wipe at my neck, did he leave any marks? I button my shirt up to the collar as he sits back against the railing, his hard cock peeking through his open jeans. "Coming here?" he asks.

Kent stumbles into the kitchen, I see him fully now, his low-riding jeans, his tanned chest. "You're hanging out," I tell Luke, poking at the tender tip of his dick for emphasis. His eyes close at the sensation. "Come on, Luke, he's headed this way."

Somehow Luke manages to cram himself into his jeans. Not bothering with his boxers, he just buttons his fly and pushes down the erection that tents through the gaping zipper. That brings another moan and he rubs at himself, he's as bad as I am. "So close," he sighs. From the kitchen I hear the crush of a beer can, the clatter of aluminum tossed into the trash, feet shuffling along the tile floor. Holding his thumb and forefinger an inch apart in front of my face, he tells me, "Marcus, I was *this*—"

Kent pushes through the screen door and steps out onto the porch.

I shove Luke's hand away. "Hey babe," I say, giving Kent a tight grin that he doesn't return. Stepping over my legs, he sinks into one of the wicker chairs across from us, sets his beer mug on the table beside him with a jarring *chink* of glass on glass.

As Luke pulls his legs up to his chest and out of Kent's way, a strategic maneuver to hide the erection still straining the front of his jeans, I try to calm my racing blood and beating heart, try to erase the memory of Luke's lips on my skin, his dick in my hand, and I'm hoping I sound nonchalant and not the least bit guilty when I ask Kent, "So what's up?"

He grunts in reply. "Thought you were going for a walk," he mutters.

"We did," I say, and Luke adds, "A short one."

Kent looks around the porch, out over the stunted grass that stretches between the house and his produce lot, out at the road. His eyes are dark, unreadable beneath the brim of his hat. I don't realize I'm holding my breath until he speaks my name. Looking up at him, staring off past us into the night, I ask, "Yeah?"

He nudges his half-empty mug with the back of his hand. "Get me a beer, will you?"

Anger floods through me. He interrupted us for *that?* "You were just in there," I sigh. "Why didn't you—"

Turning towards me, his watery eyes pin me with a hard stare and he lashes out, "Just get me a fucking beer, will you?"

For a brief second I consider saying no. *Get it yourself,* but that'll just piss him off more and I'm not in the mood for him tonight. I'm in the mood for this boy beside me, and the sooner Kent drops off, the sooner we can get back to where we were a few moments ago. "Jesus," I mumble, pushing myself up off the porch. I catch Luke's sympathetic smile and roll my eyes. What was he saying about leaving tonight?

You ain't leaving just yet, a voice in me whispers, and I storm through the screen door, let it slam shut behind me, because it's true. No, I'm not walking out, but when Kent pulls shit like this I wonder if I should even bother to stick around. Who am I to him? A lackey, a servant, a sometime sex-toy, nothing more. Who'll get his beer when I'm gone? *Answer me that,* I challenge the voice in my head as I duck into the fridge for a cold can.

When I close the fridge, I hear Kent's drunken slur from outside, and at first I'm almost sure he's talking to me. "I don't like you, kid," he says loudly, as if he wants me to overhear. *Me?* I want to ask, my heart in my throat—that would make it so easy, wouldn't it? If he didn't like me anymore, if he wanted me to leave, he'd be making the decision for me, he wouldn't have to *know*—

But he's not talking to me. He means Luke, I realize this when he adds, "I don't like freeloaders." His words fade in and out like the tide, and I tiptoe up to the screen door so I can hear better. From his spot against the railing, Luke glances up at me before turning his attention back to Kent, who can't see me where I'm standing. "You run off from home," he's saying, "that's your business. Don't bring it in here. Just keep running for all I care."

Luke doesn't respond—what's there to say? *I don't like you...* I fiddle with the tab on the top of the beer can as Kent continues. "I'm only letting you stay because *he* likes you." He means me. "If it were up to me, I'd have kicked your sorry ass out the first night."

Clearing his throat, Luke folds his arms over the tops of his knees and stares at me as he asks, "I'm sorry? I don't know what you want me to—"

Kent's harsh voice interrupts him. "I know what you did this afternoon." The beer can slips from my nerveless fingers, hits the floor with a hollow thud, he knows...Luke's eyes go wide and he looks from Kent to me then back again. My mind is a whirl of incoherent thought, *he knows*— "You think I wouldn't see?" Kent goes on. "You break my goddamn wheelbarrow and think I won't notice?"

The wheelbarrow—he's not talking about...my knees go weak in relief, thank the *Lord,* he's not talking about what Luke and I did in the barn, thank God. With trembling fingers I pick up the beer can and set it on the counter. From the fridge I snag another as outside Luke starts, "I can explain, man."

"I broke that," I say, coming out onto the porch. Kent frowns up at me as I lean past him for his mug, and I give him an overly bright grin. "The wheelbarrow," I explain before he can ask. "I broke it, babe. Meant to tell you earlier but I guess it just slipped my mind. I'm sorry."

I fill his mug, set it and the can on the table, and give him a quick kiss on the forehead before sitting back down beside Luke, who looks at me with something akin to fear. I want to hold him, tell him it's alright but I can't, not with my lover right here. When Kent doesn't say anything, I give him another smile and promise, "I'll fix it in the morning. Just needs a splint, it won't take long."

Kent stares into his mug and mumbles, "I still don't like him." As if

Luke's not sitting next to me, as if he can't hear every word that's said.

"He's pulling his share," I point out. "Helping out in the fields? And he's a good cook." *And he loves me in a way you won't or can't,* I add silently. *I don't care if you like him or not, he's mine.*

Taking a swig of his beer, Kent doesn't respond.

❋

IT SEEMS LIKE HOURS pass before Kent starts to nod off. With him sitting right in front of us, I don't dare say much to Luke, I don't smile at him or even look his way, not when every fiber of my being is screaming for his touch. Kent will see the desire in my eyes if I look at the boy, he'll hear the lust in my voice. It's only from the corner of my vision that I see Luke, his knees pulled up to his chest, arms crossed and chin resting on his wrist, and when he speaks, it's in clipped tones that belie the excitement I know must still course through his blood.

"Fix the wheelbarrow tomorrow," he says, and I nod, yes, we'll do that. He laughs nervously, runs a hand through his hair to push it from his eyes, glances at Kent and then looks away into the night. "Doesn't like me none. Why am I not surprised?"

I look up at my lover, sure he's heard the remark, but his chin rests on his chest and he's begun that wet snore he has that tells me he's out for the night. With my hand on Luke's arm, I push myself up from the porch and grin down at him when he looks at me. "*I* like you," I whisper. That makes him smile. Now that Kent's more or less asleep, I can tousle Luke's hair and kiss the top of his head. I'm only half-kidding when I add, "He's just jealous."

And there's Luke's sunny grin. I offer him my hand to help him stand, and as he wipes the dust off his butt, I turn to Kent. This is old hat now, one hand beneath either arm, haul him to his feet, murmur comfortingly when he starts. "It's okay, babe," I say, holding my breath to keep from getting a good whiff of acrid sweat and stale beer. "Come on, Kent. Time for bed."

He mutters something incoherent and swats at his mug, which Luke grabs up from the table before he can knock it to the floor. Then Kent leans against me, heavy and awkward, and I stagger back beneath his sudden weight. "Hon, come on." I say, steering him to the doorway. I hear a splash as Luke tosses the beer out into the grass and then we're inside, the screen door slapping shut behind us. Kent's arms are hot in my hands, his bare chest and back like fire beneath my touch. "Are you okay?" I ask as I lead him down the hall to his bedroom. My fingers brush against his forehead and come away sweaty and warm. "Kent, you're burning up. Are you—"

"Fine," he grumbles, pushing me away. His hands claw at my shirt, my waist, and somehow he trips over his own feet and pins me to the wall. I groan his name, shove him off me, but he fingers my belt, my zipper, feels the hardness at my groin, the erection that lingers from the few stolen moments with Luke. In the darkness of the hall, Kent leans into my face, his breath like a furnace along my skin. "Marcus," he sighs, digging into my crotch. He giggles drunkenly, presses me back against the wall, his hips grinding into mine. "You little fox."

"Kent?" I ask. Easing my hands between us, I push against him but he doesn't budge. *Please don't want to fuck tonight,* I pray. I don't want him, I want Luke. *Please don't, Kent, just please*—he tries to kiss me but I turn away, and his damp lips smear across my cheek as he laughs breathlessly in my ear. I want to call out to Luke, I don't want Kent, *please...* "Baby?" I try, sidestepping away from him. "I don't think you're really up for it tonight, you know? Maybe tomorrow, what do you say?"

I break away from him but he's quick, he grabs me around the waist and hugs me back to him, this is *fun* for him. "You want it now," he slurs, groping at my crotch, and it takes everything I have not to hurt him to get away. *Not from you,* I think, but I can't say that, he doesn't know and now isn't the time to tell him, not with so much alcohol in his system. In the morning, I promise myself, after we've both had a good night's sleep but not now and sure as hell not when he's in this sort of mood...

"Marcus!" he curses as I stumble out of his grip. I make it to the end of the hall, him right behind me every step of the way, and as I push the door to his room open, I hear his jeans hit the floor. I turn to find him half-naked in the hall, his briefs pulled down below the thick erection that stands up from pale skin and dense hair between his legs.

"Damn it, kid," he mutters, encircling his shaft with one hand. He steps towards me, closing the distance between us, his hand working at his dick and he's going to want some release, I've known him too long not to see what's coming next. Me bent over the foot of his bed, him thrusting into me a few times, what'll it hurt? We've done it before.

Before Luke, I think, stepping into Kent's bedroom as he advances on me. Luke said he's cool with how I feel for Kent but right now I don't *want* this, I don't want just sex, I don't want *him.* I look past him down the hall at the boy watching us from the living room and *he's* what I want—how did I get myself into this?

When Kent's in the room, I close the door behind him, I don't want

Luke watching. This won't do anything for me—I feel like a condemned man, I don't want to do this, but I have to. I must. A few thrusts and Kent will be done. We've done it before. Then Luke's hands and lips can wash the memory away, and in the morning I'll talk with Kent, I'll tell him about Luke and how it is between us, and all this will be over. Another couple hours, I can make it that long. I must.

But Kent's more tired than aroused, and before I even get my jeans unbuckled, he's facedown in his pillows, one hand still squeezing his swollen length as he starts to snore. "Thank you," I murmur. Staring down at him, I feel used and dirty and horrible, simply unclean. My hands shake at the thought of what Kent wanted, I feel nauseous and sick, sex with *him*? After that wondrous time with Luke in the barn? After what we had last night? I want to throw up, I'm so disgusted at myself.

Luke is waiting for me.

I manage to get Kent's boots off, his jeans, his hat—I toy with the idea of taking the briefs off, as well, but that would mean touching his ass and cock and I don't want to do that. So I settle for throwing the sheets over his legs and I almost kill myself when I stumble over his boots. If I were a drinking man, I'd consider a glass of whatever Kent has in those bottles beneath the sink, anything to calm my stomach and soothe my nerves. *That's what I have Luke for,* I tell myself as I open the bedroom door just wide enough to slip out.

✻

I HEAD FOR THE porch but Luke has other plans. He meets me in the kitchen doorway and, taking my hand, leads me back down the hall. Through Kent's closed door I can hear his rumbling snores, like thunder in the night. Then we're in my own room, and Luke shuts the door behind us, throws the lock, the sound is loud in the darkness.

Gently he guides me to the bed, clicks on the lamp by his flower, which is open like a heart in bloom—diffused light pushes back the shadows, rims the petals with golden dust. I sit on the edge of the bed and stare at that flower, those petals, red as blood. "I have to tell him," I whisper. I feel Luke's hand on my face and I lean into his touch, so warm, so alive. Squeezing my eyes shut, I press my lips into his palm. "God, I'm sorry," I sigh. "I'm just...I mean—"

"I know," he assures me, and his gentle hand tells me that yes, he *does* know. *I love you,* I want to say, but I'm afraid it's too soon, I'm technically still with Kent. I should just call it a night and go to sleep. As if reading my mind, Luke tells me, "Lie down."

His voice is soft like his hands. In the dusky lamplight, the buttons of my shirt disappear beneath his fingers. I let him ease the shirt off my shoulders and down my arms, his touch golden on my skin. Then those hands are at my waist, unzipping my jeans, pushing them to the floor as well, my boxers too, until I stand naked before him. "Marcus," he sighs, my name amazing in his voice. He kisses my bare thighs, my hips, my stomach, as his hands guide me onto the bed. The sheets are cool against my skin, the pillow like a dream I've had before, I simply melt into it again. I'll feel better in the morning, I'm sure of it.

Luke's hands trace the outline of my body through the covers, and when I look at him, he's so close, his face draped in shadow because his shoulder blocks the light. His lips touch mine, a brief kiss, and he whispers, "I want to love you, Marcus. I want to stay here tonight and hold you but if it's not the right time yet, let me know. I'll do what you want me to do. Just let me know."

I should thank him and turn him away. But he's what I want, more than anything else—I've been aching for him all night, I've been living for this moment, my head tells me I should just go to sleep but my heart, my body, beg to differ. "Luke," I breathe, and that's as far as I get before his mouth covers mine, his tongue licks into me, the sweetest goodnight kiss I've had in years. "You can stay."

He steps back from the bed and pulls his shirt off over his head, drops it to the floor. He unbuttons the fly on his jeans and slips them and his boxers down in one motion, kicks them away as he climbs over me into the bed. For the few dear moments he's above me, the covers are the only thing keeping us apart, and his weight is so delicious that I roll over beneath him just to feel as much of his body press against as much of mine as I possibly can.

Then he's sliding beneath the sheets, his naked body finally lying alongside mine, and I feel like this is my first time with a boy, I feel trembly and anxious and I could come just looking at him leaning over me. He brushes the hair back from my face, kisses the corner of my eye, whispers that he thinks I'm lovely. *Lovely,* I'm sure Kent doesn't even *know* that word.

I close my eyes as Luke's hands trace the curve of my jaw, down my throat, down my chest and lower, until his fingers coil in the hair at my groin and *lower,* until he's touching the tender flesh he licked this afternoon, and the memory of that makes me pull him down to me for a hungry kiss, three, a dozen. His breath is mine, his words lost in me.

It's like a slow dance, him moving above me while I follow his lead, my leg draped around his hip, the hardness at his crotch pressing into me. Kent doesn't do it like this, this easy, this unhurried, each movement deliberate, each kiss lingering, his hands holding me back against the pillow and his lips, his mouth, his tongue and fingers rubbing me until I have to bite into his shoulder to keep from crying out. When Luke enters me, he presses me to the mattress, his whole body covering me, his heart thudding against mine, his arms holding me to him like a precious memory.

I'm used to Kent's rapid thrusts, his pulling out before the deed is done—I'm not at all prepared for Luke. He thrusts into me once, so far inside that I'm sure he'll pull out and ram back in, that's how Kent does it, I'm waiting for that…but it's not his way. Instead, he stays inside, moves within me in an almost circular motion, tiny little thrusts that send slivers of pleasure shooting through me and dig him in further, deeper, his nails scratching at my back as he moans in my ear, *uh uh uh* in rhythm with his dick.

My own erection throbs between us, and each small thrust rubs his lower belly against my cock, crushes my balls, until I'm sure I'm going to come, I *have* to. He pulls out slightly like a reprieve, then shoves back in, deeper than before, is that *possible?* He's reaching into parts of me I've never let anyone touch, he's bringing me to a climax that I'm sure will tear the roof off, rip me apart with desire, leave me whimpering and weak like a child in his arms. I raise up on my elbows, push against him, meet him thrust for thrust, *uh uh uh,* a breathless mantra that makes me grip his ass, raise my knees, flex my muscles until he's so far in, he'll never find his way out.

And then, one final shove and he comes, fire racing through my groin and flooding into me. He sighs my name, presses me back against the bed, moves above me until the sensation of him in me explodes in an orgasm that drowns out every lover I've ever had. There is no other, he's the only one.

With his soft lips on mine I break down and tell him I love him because I do.

※

I CRY AFTERWARDS, LIKE he's my first. Luke holds me, murmurs into my hair, it'll be alright, it's okay, and I believe him. It's going to be okay.

Sometime before the sun rises, I wake to find him climbing over me. "What?" I ask, groggy with sleep. The room is a washed-out morning gray that tells me it's too damn early to be up. I grasp at the blankets covering us to hold him before he can slip away. "Where are you going?"

He kisses my jaw, noses the hair away from in front of my ear and whispers, "The couch."

I'm more awake now, and when he tries to slide out of bed, I won't let him. "Luke." I speak in the same whispered tones that he uses, as if Kent's asleep in the room with us and we don't want to wake him. "No…"

He kisses me again—so persuasive, his kisses. "It's still early," he explains, his words mere breath that tickles my neck as he nuzzles against me. His arms are strong around me, I had almost forgotten what it felt like to wake beside another's warm body. "If I get to the couch now, Kent won't know I was here. You want to tell him yourself, right?" I nod into his shoulder, my hands fisting at his back, unwilling to let him go. "You don't want him to find the couch empty," Luke reasons—yes, I realize that would be a bad thing. "It's just for a few hours, Marcus. I love you."

I haven't heard that one in years. "Then love me now," I whisper, clinging to him. Before he can reply, I stroke his leg with one foot, press my knee into his crotch, bite at his earlobe and moan into him, his name, *please,* I want him again. It doesn't take much to get him aroused—he's young and hungry for someone to love him, same as me, and I'm ready for him this time, I know what to expect.

But he still surprises me, with his quick little thrusts and his slow hands, his tender kisses. He pins me to the bed like a captured butterfly, pushes into me, deeper, deeper, without pulling out deeper, and when he comes, he's so far inside that I swear I taste him in the back of my throat. He's a spark that ignites my blood, and this time I don't cry. There are no tears, no regrets, nothing but him in me and above me and pressing me to the bed with soft, persistent kisses. He tells me he loves me again, in that whispered voice he's using like he wants no one else in the entire world to overhear us, and I kiss the words from his lips. Then he says he has to go.

Almost reluctantly, I let him crawl from between the covers, and I hug the sheets to my face to breathe in his musky scent as I watch him dress. He kisses my forehead like an indulgent parent, tousles my hair, trails his hand over the blankets and down the curve of my spine, and I sit up just enough to land his next kiss on my mouth. I had almost forgotten this post-coital play could exist, him giggling against my lips, me reluctant to let him go.

But another hour or so and Kent will be up. So Luke leaves my room, closing the door quietly behind himself, and suddenly I'm alone again, almost cold. I huddle into blankets that still smell like him and stare at his flower as I drift back to sleep.

※

THE DAISY IS THE first thing I see when I wake up a second time. The stem's just beginning to droop in the early morning light, and most of the water in the glass has evaporated, no wonder the flower's dying. I almost want to press the petals between the pages of a book, or maybe in my folder full of cowboy ads, anything to keep it. But I don't need just the flower: I have the boy who gave it to me, and he'll give me a hundred more if I only ask. *As long as they're not from Kent's garden,* I think, smiling wryly at myself as I throw the covers back and climb out of bed.

Luke's shirt is still on my bedroom floor. I'm tempted to pull it on, it's mine and probably smells like him, I could wear it and feel him holding me again. But I think of Kent—he'll notice the shirt, he'd recognize it as the one Luke wore yesterday, and I don't want to clue him in before I get a chance to talk to him about…well, about us. About how we're through.

Are we through?

We have to be, I reason. Whatever Kent and I once had is gone now, isn't it? I went further than flirtatious talk over breakfast, hidden hands thrust beneath clothing, kisses on the couch and a blowjob in the barn. Last night, with Luke? How can Kent and I *not* be through after that?

But here in the bright light of dawn, what happened last night almost seems like a dream. Wonderful, heady, the type of dream so amazing, so *real,* that your heart aches to find upon awakening it isn't true. *But this one is,* I tell myself. I look at the tousled sheets that kept Luke close to me while we slept, I look at the daisy and the shirt on my floor. I could open the bedroom door, glance down the hall to see him curled up on the couch but the truth is that boy is real. What we did last night, what we *felt,* is true.

And what about Kent? a voice inside me wants to know. *He's real too, isn't he?* Larger than life when sober, heart of stone, but he's sheltered me these past two years, fed me, clothed me, fucked me in some semblance of affection, if not love. Am I ready to discard all that?

With a pang of regret, some small part of me thinks maybe last night was a mistake. *No,* I tell myself, *nothing with Luke is wrong*—but maybe I should've held back, maybe I should've waited until I had worked everything out with Kent first before I moved on. I have to tell him about Luke, today, now, right this minute. I have to tell him, *Look, this is how it is…*

And how *is* it, exactly?

I love Luke. I know this with every pore of my being, he's a dream I never want to wake from if I can help it. I love his hands on my body, his lips on mine, his eyes that hold such desire and naked lust when he looks my way that my mind simply overloads. He loves me, he said it first thing this morning, he loves *me.*

That contrary voice inside of me whispers, *And doesn't Kent?*

He's never said the word out loud.

So what, that means he doesn't? I shake my head to clear it, I don't know the answer to that. I don't know how I feel about him any more, or where things stand between us. In Luke's arms it all seems so easy, my emotions are drawn out in black and white. Last night I was so sure that I had to leave, there was no other choice. But the morning sun casts shadows of doubt over my feelings, and grey uncertainty clouds my mind, smudging my resolve. I could go into the kitchen now and glance out the window, see Kent in his black cowboy hat, and fall for him all over again. One look at Luke asleep on the couch and I'd be lost for him, too. So who is it I *really* love?

Cautiously I open the door to my bedroom and peer out. One of Luke's feet sticks from beneath the blankets on the couch but he doesn't snore so I can't tell if he's asleep or not. *Please don't see me,* I pray, tiptoeing out into the hallway. I need a few moments to myself to figure out what I'm thinking, what I'm feeling, what I'm going to do next, and those violet eyes would only make the decision for me.

Down the other end of the hall, Kent's bedroom door is ajar—he's up, probably out in his market already, watering the plants. Without alcohol to dull his senses, would he see my guilt written plainly across my face? Would he take one look at me and just know I didn't sleep alone last night? Would he care?

I need a shower to wash all the doubts away. But when I click on the light, the bathroom is too sterile, too white, so damn bright that it hurts my head. In the shower stall, the hot water sears my skin. What am I doing here? Playing with fire, dangling Kent while I fuck around with Luke, all this clandestine shit, I'm just begging to be burned. What if Kent wasn't so drunk last night? How could I have had sex with him knowing Luke waited for me? Would I have gone from one to the other like a common whore?

Look what you've done, I tell myself. I hate that voice, the one inside my head. In the stark bathroom, it's loud enough to drown out the shower's rush. *How can Kent live without you? He'll drink himself to death and it'll be your fault. You bitch that he doesn't love you but do you really love him? For who he is, not who you want him to be? You've made him into one of the guys in your magazine ads, a two-dimensional caricature of what you think a cowboy should be. Of course he can't live up to that. No one could. You don't love him…how the hell can you expect anything in return?*

I don't know. *How can you love Luke?* that voice continues. *If you paint him in the same light, how can you love someone who doesn't really exist?*

I don't *know.* I tell myself it's different with Luke, *he's* different, it's real what we have together in a way it never was with Kent. Luke's searching for something in me just the same as I'm looking for that cowboy in him, isn't he?

I'm not so sure anymore. Around me hot water rains down like brimstone and I don't know who I love, what I want, I don't know shit. I sink to the tiled floor, my weight bringing me down, and I burrow into my arms, pull my knees to my chest, make myself as tiny as possible and still the water stings me, it beats my face and stains my flesh. One or the other, I have to choose.

I can't have both.

pART 4

Luke finds me curled into one corner of the shower. I don't even realize he's there until the water cuts off and he drapes a towel around my shoulders, helping me to my feet. "Marcus, what's wrong?" he wants to know, rubbing the towel down my arms, my legs, my chest. Concern laces his violet eyes, tightens his mouth into a thin white line. "Talk to me," he pleads as he dries me off. "Are you okay? Are you—"

"I'm fine," I whisper, but my words are lost in the rasp of the towel on my skin and I don't think he believes me, anyway. He wraps the towel around me, holds me close, won't let me go when I try to pull away. "I'm fine," I assure him, my voice strengthening. His arms tighten around me and in that moment, my mind is made up. Like the sun breaking through an overcast sky, my mind clears for the first time in days. With Luke here with me, I really *am* fine. *You win,* I want to say but don't—I couldn't begin to explain what all I've been going through inside since he came into my life. But the battle's over, Luke has won, whether he knows it or not, because he came for me, *him,* and Kent did not.

Drying my hair, Luke holds the sides of my head so I have to look up at him, and he won't let me look away. "If everything's fine, then what's the matter?" he asks. He punctuates the question with a kiss right between my eyebrows.

Cowboy

"I'm just…" I sigh, fisting my hand in the towel, wiping my eyes. "I've got to tell Kent," I admit. My voice is muffled by the towel in front of my face.

Luke holds me, his arms giving me the strength I need and I lean against him, so warm, so dry, so *safe*. He feels so safe to me. "What are you going to say?" he asks. That's a good one—I don't know. "Marcus?"

"It's all my fault," I say. Luke shakes his head but the words tumble free, I can't stop them. "It's all my fault, I'll tell him that, and I'm sorry, alright? I'm sorry I don't love him anymore. If I ever did." I *know* I did, I had to have, once. "But I'm with you now. He has to see this. He has to know."

I sink into Luke's arms and hide my face in his shirt, where he smells clean and wonderful, and I let him hold me close, I let his hands on my back calm me. I'm not sure how long we stand like this, in each other's arms in the middle of the bathroom, but I don't want to move, I don't want to lose this, lose *him*. I want this moment to last forever.

✫

IN MY BEDROOM, I dress quickly in jeans and a faded t-shirt. Luke sits on the bed in his boxers, watching me, listening. "I'll talk to Kent," I say, more to myself than to him, trying to boost my courage. I can do this. "I'll say look, this is how things are, and he'll listen." He hasn't been drinking much yet, he'll hear me out. It'll be alright, I tell myself. He has to have seen this coming.

I lead Luke out into the hallway, the house around us quiet. Far off I hear the sound of running water—Kent already hosing down his plants, he must've left the kitchen door open if I can hear him from here. Dread rises in me, I don't want to do this, I don't want to say a word…I reach out behind me and Luke catches my wrist, entwines his fingers with mine. "You sure you want to tell him right this minute?" he asks.

I nod. I have to tell him now, before the customers arrive. *While he's still sober.* I don't have to say the words, Luke nods as if he's thinking them himself. "I just want you to be ready," I say, and he nods again. I'm not sure what's going to happen, if Kent will get angry and throw us out, if he'll at least let me pack, I just don't know, but I want Luke to be prepared for anything.

"Do you want me to come with you?" he asks, giving my hand a comforting squeeze.

To be honest, I'd love for him to be by my side, it'd put my mind at rest and make this whole thing that much easier, but it wouldn't be fair to

Kent. None of this is fair, really, me falling for this wonderful boy beneath his roof, kissing on him and sexing him up when my lover's at home. *Ex-lover,* I remind myself, but it doesn't make me feel any less guilty. If Luke comes with me now, Kent will think we're ganging up on him, and I don't want that. I want this whole thing over with as quickly as possible—I want this to go smoothly, I want us to part as friends.

I hope we can part as friends.

Shaking my head, I tell Luke, "No, it's okay." With a nod back at my bedroom, I ask, "Just get dressed, please? In case."

He nods and as he releases my sweaty hand, I wipe it on my jeans. "It's okay," he assures me, kissing my cheek. His hand on my back is so comforting, I just want to lean into his touch and never resurface. "I'm here for you, Marcus," he says. His lips crush mine in a velvet kiss. "I love you."

I can do this. With him behind me, waiting for me, I can talk to Kent. I must.

Pointing towards the living room, where he slept, I ask, "Can you get the sheets off the couch?"

Luke nods. "Sure."

Suddenly a million chores buzz through my mind, things that need to be done before I leave, things Kent won't think to do on his own. "Run them through the wash," I tell him, and Luke nods again. "My clothes, too, the dirty ones. And the towel on my floor."

"Okay." Ever eager to please, Luke rubs my back as he watches me closely. "Anything else?"

"I just want things neat here," I tell him. I don't want to leave a mess behind. There's a part of me that somehow hopes that if I tidy the house and get it in order, then maybe things will go smoother with Kent.

"I know," Luke assures me. "I'll clean up. You just go talk to him, okay?"

Okay. I can do that. "Can you get a few of my things together?" I ask. I hate the worry eating at me, I hate this indecision, this not knowing. "I mean, just in case—"

"Sure." With a quick kiss, Luke grins and says, "You're stalling."

I give him a wan smile and nod, determined. "I know." He gives me a slight push in the direction of the kitchen. I let my feet take over from there.

At the screen door, I look out and see Kent in his market, hose in hand, black jeans, black hat, bare tanned back. From here he reminds me of those silhouettes some people have in their yards, black cutouts of a cowboy leaning against the side of the house, arms folded, head ducked down, one knee up like he's just waiting. Waiting…I get the feeling Kent's waiting for me, he knows what's coming, he *has* to know. The flirtatious looks, the coy words, the laughter—how could he miss that? How could he not know what Luke is to me?

Coffee, I think, it's ingrained in me, I bring his coffee. Because it buys me some time, I brew a quick pot, and as it percolates, I play out the coming scene in my mind. I'll take him a cup, like I do every morning. With a nonchalant shrug, I'll shove my hands deep into the pockets of my jeans, rock back on my heels just slightly, stare out at the plants or the road or maybe even further, out to the horizon, where a thin haze blurs the boundary between earth and sky. I'll clear my throat so my voice is sure and strong when I tell him we have to talk. *We have to talk*—that's how it always starts, doesn't it? The beginning of the end.

He'll know what I want. In my mind, I believe it's that easy, he'll turn and see the look in my eyes and just *know* that we're through, I won't have to say the words. I won't have to tell him that Luke is a better lover than he is, I won't have to cuckold him with any intimate details. Maybe he'll wish me luck, me and my boy. Maybe he'll dig out the money in his back pocket, peel a few twenties off the roll that I know he's saving for drink, shove the bills into my hand and shake his head when I try to give it back.

Hell, while I'm dreaming? Maybe he'll drive us into town, why not? Drop us off at the bus station, get us tickets to the coast, I'll surprise Ally with a knock on her door and this time tomorrow I'll be introducing her to Luke. *See?* I think, imagining the look on my sister's face when she finds I've brought an honest-to-God cowboy with me. *Found one after all.*

Daydreams, that's all they are. I'm stalling again. The coffee's brewed—I pour a steaming mug and drop a few ice cubes into the hot liquid to cool it off. Then I take a deep breath, another one, a third…will they help? I don't feel any steadier, and my hand trembles when I pick up the mug, I have to hold it in both hands so I don't splash the coffee. I hear Luke in the shower and tell myself I can do this. I *have* to.

Mug in hand, I push through the screen door and step outside.

✻

I STUMBLE BAREFOOT OVER the gravel but Kent doesn't look up as I approach. I don't expect him to. Coming up behind him, I hold the mug out like I always do. "Your coffee," I tell him. I have to bite back all the other words I'm aching to say.

He takes the offered drink without looking my way—he doesn't see me, I don't exist for him. It's just the plants and the hose and the road ahead, the steaming java that warms his face as he gulps it down. I wait until he lowers the mug, then clear my throat. *We have to talk*...I know what I have to say, I know the words, but they won't come free. "Kent?" I ask. I hate the trepidatious quiver in my voice.

He doesn't answer, no surprise there. Just a tilt of his head to indicate he's heard me at all. Water keeps streaming from the hose in a steady rush that rains over hibiscus flowers and potted rhododendrons, holly bushes, marigolds. Kent has a way with plants that never ceases to amaze me—he can eke beautiful greenery from the dry desert sand, orchestrate foliage in this bitter sun, paint this cracked landscape with his palette of flowers and vegetables, but he can't touch me that way, he can't make *me* bloom...is that somehow my fault? Is there something wrong with *me*—am I just as blind as he is in this relationship? "Kent," I sigh. This time he sort of almost turns to me, I can see him looking from the corner of his eye. "We need to talk."

Here's where he tells me he knows, he's been meaning to say something to me. I fool myself into thinking that my heart is hardened against what's coming, I'm prepared. He knows I love Luke and we part as friends, that's the script I'm reading from right now.

Only he must be on a different page or something, because with a lusty sigh he throws his head back, downs the rest of the coffee, then sets the cup on a nearby vegetable stand so hard that I can hear the ceramic rattle over the flow of water. "Marcus," he says, weary and old, "if this is about last night, I don't want to hear it."

Last night—Luke in my bed, loving me, holding me, did he know about that? Before I can ask, he hurries on, exasperated. I haven't been awake a full hour yet and already he's fed up with me. "You know how tired I get," he tells me, spraying the hose over his plants. Not once has he ever turned that playful spray onto me.

He's never seen the cool water plaster my t-shirt to my chest, harden my nipples, trickle down my arms and darken my jeans. "I work out here in the hot sun every day and all I ask for is a little time to myself in the evenings to unwind, you know, kid? I've got needs, too. You can't expect me to put out all the damn time."

He's talking about sex. Somehow he's convinced himself that I was the one who wanted it last night, I was the one who pressured him into dropping his drawers in the hallway, and he thinks I'm mad because he fell asleep before we did anything.

"Maybe later," he's saying, still not looking my way. "We didn't connect last night and I know you're pissed about that, but it happens. You can't screw all the damn time, Marcus. You have to start thinking with the head on your shoulders and not the one between—"

"It's over," I say, interrupting him. He stops in mid-sentence, a frown already tugging at his lips, and I close my eyes against the fear and sorrow warring in my heart. "Kent, I'm...I'm sorry."

"Over." He says the word like he's never heard it before. I nod but I know he doesn't see me, I don't have to open my eyes to know he's still frowning out over his damn plants. "Marcus—"

"Over," I repeat, and the word echoes in me like a nail hammered into the lid of a coffin, *over.* "Between us. I'm...Kent, I'm sorry." I don't know what else to say. "I just—I don't think this is what I want." *This meaning you,* I add silently. Maybe if I'm lucky, I can play this off like I'm just an unsatisfied lover, I won't have to bring Luke into it at all...

But Kent isn't stupid, he knows what's going on, he *has* to. I'm fine for two years—a little disgruntled, perhaps, a little under-loved, a little under-appreciated, but at least I was more or less satisfied. Then Luke shows up, I'm jacking off all over the place like a teenager in heat, mooning and fawning over the boy and now I want out? "It's him," Kent says, disgusted. I squeeze my eyes shut tighter, hoping this will all go away. The water cuts off and I can feel the heat of his gaze on me, how many beers has he had already today? With something that almost sounds like a laugh, he mutters, "I should've seen it coming."

My lower lip trembles and I promise myself I won't cry, but when I look at him, I see disbelief in his eyes, mingled with a pain I put there, and I feel tears clog the back of my throat. "I'm sorry," I say again, as ineffectual as that sounds, but I am, God I am, so damn sorry I've hurt him like this. Reaching out, I touch his arm. "Kent—"

He jerks away from me and my fingers curl into a useless fist. "I thought he was nothing to worry about," he spits—my own words thrown back at me. How long has it been since I said that? And even then I was lying, I knew I wanted Luke, I knew I needed him the same way I need the sun to live, the air to breathe. "I thought you said he'd move on soon enough. How long have you been lying to me, Marcus?"

"It's not like that," I tell him, but I know he doesn't believe me, it's in the hardened set of his jaw, his steely eyes. "Kent, please, listen. He loves me—"

Turning away, he counters, "And you think I don't?"

And you think... "Kent," I sob. "I don't know what to think." My thoughts are bound out in a whirlwind that threatens to swallow me whole, a twister that will tear me to pieces in its wake. *Too late,* I think. *Oh God, too damn late.* Quietly, so he won't hear the emotion that chokes me, I whisper,

"I'm in love with him, too. I think...I think I should just leave."

Kent spins around, anger clouding his face. I'm about to apologize again, somehow that *has* to help, when he pegs the empty mug at me. I try to shield myself but it hits my elbow with a dull *thock!* and then falls to the ground, shattering on the stones at my feet. Ceramic shards cut into my ankles as I jump back, he threw that at me, my arm stings and my hand's gone numb and he actually *threw* it... "So it's like that," he mutters, anger hardening his voice. "Just up and leave, don't give a damn about me. Find someone new to fuck and move on, is that it?"

I shake my head, no. "It's not—" I try, but he flicks the hose at me, thumbs the nozzle on, and a splash of cold water hits me in the center of my chest like a bullet. I look at him in shock—this isn't how it's supposed to go. This isn't what I hoped for, what I *wanted*. After two years together, we can at least reason this out, right?

Apparently not. Kent's not listening to me. Another shot with the hose, this one higher, I feel the spray fleck my neck and chin, and he tells me, "So leave already. Get your shit together and get the fuck out of here, if that's what you want to do."

I don't want it to end like this. "Kent—"

He turns away, veins in his neck and face standing like cords beneath his skin. "I'm through with you," he says.

I turn and race for the house.

✻

I BURST THROUGH THE screen door and into the kitchen, tears that I refuse to cry blurring my vision into a kaleidoscope of colors and shapes that mean nothing to me. Kent's words still echo in my ears—*and you think I don't?* Jesus, what the hell was I *supposed* to think? He's never said he loved me, he does nothing to drive the point home, he thinks a halfhearted fuck and a place to live is enough to show me he cares? How could I *not* fall for Luke, when he can't stop touching me and he holds me tight long after we both come, and he tells me he loves me? How can I not want to hear the words?

Through the living room, down the hall, I push into my room and slam the door shut behind me, *fuck*. This isn't what I wanted, the hatred I saw in Kent's eyes, the anger and disbelief and pain. I assumed he knew what was going on, I've dropped enough hints, I've told him outright it's his drinking that pisses me off, that was our last fight, how could he still manage to look so damn incredulous and hurt when I told him I love Luke?

And if I truly don't love Kent anymore, why does my heart feel like it's being torn in two?

Luke's still in my room, rummaging through the drawers of my dresser. On the freshly made bed are a few t-shirts, folded into a neat stack on the covers. I catch a glimpse of my folder full of ads beneath the shirts, and somehow that makes this all real, that makes it hurt worse. That Luke would think to pack *that,* when Kent doesn't even know about it…I sink to the edge of the bed and rub my elbow, which stings from the mug Kent threw, and struggle not to cry.

"How'd it go?" Luke asks me. When I don't answer, he turns and sees me, and something in my face makes him drop the jeans in his hand and come to my side. "Marcus," he murmurs, taking me into his arms—so strong, so young. What are we going to do? Where will we go? I have nothing and he doesn't really have all that much more. Somehow I always thought I'd be farther than this by now. Concern laces Luke's voice as he asks, "What happened?"

I can't speak above a whisper, and my words are muffled against Luke's shirt. "He told me to get out," I tell him.

He sits back, cradles my face in both of his large hands, and studies me until I can't bear the look of love staring back from those purple eyes, I'm not used to it, I have to look away. "Marcus," he sighs. The tenderness in his voice is enough to bring a fresh onslaught of tears. Gently he kisses me, his lips barely touching mine. "I'm right here. We're in this together, I'm not leaving you."

I pretend his kisses, his hands, will make everything alright.

✱

JEANS AND SOCKS AND boxers, t-shirts, shorts, button-down shirts that Luke favors, I take everything out of the dresser, the closet, pile it all on bed. "I'm not sure we can take this much," Luke tells me, picking up each item of clothing to fold it to one side. "When I left my house, I just had the clothes on my back. This…" He gestures at the bed with a bewildered expression on his face. "I don't think we can carry it all. Do you have a bag?"

"No." My reply is terse—I'm all cried out. Kent wants to end things like this? Fine. I'll play his game, I'll be the villain, *fine.* Let him think I've wounded him, let him ignore my own scars, two years of living with a man steadily drinking himself to death, that's worn me down more than I care to admit.

But you're not mad at Luke, I remind myself. No, I'm not. With a sigh, I whisper, "I'm sorry, I'm just…on edge, I guess. I don't mean to take it out on you."

From the corner of my eye I see Luke frown at me, but he nods and murmurs, "I know." Then he goes back to folding my clothes—there *are* a lot of them.

Digging through the dresser drawers to make sure I have everything, I tell him, "Maybe we won't take it all, I don't know. This is still sort of new to me."

Far off I hear the slam of the screen door when Kent comes into the house, heavy boots clomping on hardwood floors, and before I can even think, the door to my room is kicked in and Kent is there, glaring at me. His red face and chest make him seem angrier than God in the Old Testament, he looks positively *livid,* and my fear comes flooding back. "Marcus!" he barks, my name in his voice, it almost brings me to my knees. But he notices Luke, standing wide-eyed at the bed with my clothes in his hands, and without another word Kent turns and storms from the room.

Luke and I exchange a worried glance. "What's he want?" I ask, as if he might know.

With a shrug, Luke looks at the open door, the empty hall beyond. "Maybe you should go find out," he tells me.

I don't want to know. Kent's still too damn *furious* to talk reasonably—I don't like him in this mood, I don't like that *I'm* the one who put him in it, but Luke's right, I should find out. As I hurry after Kent, I hear door hinges screech in protest as he shoves through the screen door. I follow him out to the porch, sure he'll just troop back to his market and there are already one or two cars pulled into our drive, I won't be able to talk to him there, if he even *wants* to talk.

So it's a surprise when he stops, leans out over the railing, and glares at his market, his shoulders bunched in anger. "Kent?" I ask carefully. *You okay?* I almost ask, but wouldn't *that* be a stupid question? Of course he's not okay, I'm leaving him. When it's obvious he's not going to speak first, though, I ask, "Did you want to talk to me, or something?"

"You're leaving," he says, his voice unnatural and strained. "Just like that."

He told me to get out, didn't he? "You said—"

"What, you've been packed for this?" he asks. He doesn't look at me, just stares out at the few customers already milling around his plants. "All ready to go, is that it?"

I shake my head, a gesture he doesn't see. "No, I...this is just as sudden for me, Kent, you have to believe me. I love him."

That gets a bitter laugh. "Love," Kent mutters, like he might have

Cowboy 111

heard the word once but he's not quite sure where. "You just met him, or was that a lie, too? How long have you been fucking around with him?"

Leaning against the post, I cross my arms and study the dusty wooden slats beneath my feet. Now I'm the cardboard cutout, I'm the cowboy silhouette. I can see Luke on the other side of the screen door, hovering in the darkness of the kitchen, listening to us, waiting to see if he has to step in. "I met him the way I told you I did," I say to Kent, who rolls his eyes and doesn't respond. "The day you went into town, I found him in the barn."

"And you fucked him then?" Kent asks.

I tamp down the anger that boils beneath my skin. "No."

Now Kent looks at me, and his eyes are bleary with something a lot stronger than the coffee I gave him this morning. With the mug broken, I bet he just drank straight from the flask in his pocket, it's probably empty now. So this emotion held in check, I have the alcohol to thank for that. "*Did* you fuck him?" Kent asks softly.

I want to lie to him. I want to shake my head and tell him no, just to preserve something between us, just to keep the hurt from his dark eyes. But I see Luke watching us, watching *me*, and I can't do that to him, I can't deny him like that. Slowly, I meet Kent's gaze and nod. "Last night," I whisper.

Kent's eyes close in defeat. "I'm sorry," I say, just to fill the silence that stretches around us like a shroud. "Kent, I'm...I love him." It's the only excuse I have.

Turning away, Kent laughs that short, bitter laugh of his again, the one I don't like because it sounds nothing like the man I've known for the past two years, it's a stranger's laugh and it scares me. "So you keep saying. But I'll tell you something. I don't really believe in love," he tells me.

I feel his words hit me in my chest, pierce my heart, *I don't really believe...* so I've been wasting my time with him? Lying to *myself* that he really does love me? "You don't..." I start, but I can't finish the thought, how can he not believe in love? "You mean you don't...you never *loved* me?"

His hands grip the railing so tight that his knuckles turn white. "I care for you," he says, speaking low as if he's afraid someone will overhear him. When he looks at me, I see that despite whatever's coursing through his system right now, whatever came out of his bottle, he's probably more sober at the moment than he has been in days. "Don't get me wrong, Marcus. I like the way you keep the house, and you have a great ass, I've told you that. But you don't get me worked up or anything. I'm just not into it."

I'm not comprehending this. "Into what?" I want to know. "Kent, I'm not sure I'm hearing you right. Not into what? Into *me*?"

With an uneasy shrug, he looks somewhere behind me as he recalls,

"You're the one who came to me, remember? I was just going to let you stay for a bit, you have a good head on your shoulders and I need someone like that to help me out here. I need someone like you to keep the money straight, you know I'm not good with it."

Tell me about it, I think, but I don't say that out loud. Instead, I bite my lower lip and tell myself I'm not hearing this—he doesn't *love* me?

"I hadn't had a piece of ass in a while," he continues, each word another nail driven deeper into my heart. "You were willing. Before long, I thought it was *all* you wanted, and if it kept you here, then I'd do it. I'm not like you, Marcus. Sure, I like to get off but it's not a daily thing for me the way it is for you."

I glance at Luke on the other side of the screen door and think I can see his thoughts written out in the shadows that drape his violet eyes. *He's just saying this to make you feel like shit,* that's what he'd tell me if he could, I can almost hear the words in his voice inside my head. *He's mad that you dicked him over and he's just doing this to get back at you. It's childish, he doesn't mean it.*

The problem is that I know Kent, I *know* he's not one to waste words. He means this, every single thing he's telling me now, he means every word of it. "I mean nothing to you?" I ask, incredulous. Then why the mug this morning, why the hose? Shit, he should be *happy* I'm leaving. "Kent—"

He sighs and takes off his cowboy hat, runs a hand through his dark hair, wavy with sweat. Then he sets the hat back on his head, a little crooked, and I fist my hands to keep from righting it. "I like you, Marcus," he tells me, but *like* isn't *love,* is it? "I care about you, don't get me wrong. If you get sick, I worry. If you're hurt, I get upset. But I'm not..."

Trailing off, he looks out at his market and when he speaks again, his voice is so low, it's almost a whisper. "I liked the partnership we had here. You working the house, the money, it let me do what I really wanted to be doing. If I ran this stint alone, I'd have no time for the plants. I'm worn out as it is when the day is done. If I had no one helping me, I'd be dead."

Because he's been frank with me, I feel no fear when I tell him, "You keep drinking like you do, you'll be dead before you know it."

I expect an angry retort, a slap across the face, anything but his slow, thoughtful nod, *that* closes my throat with tears, just when I thought I'd never cry again. "I'm not thrilled about what's happened," he murmurs, and I have to wipe at my eyes, I don't want him to see how he's gotten to me.

"I don't like being lied to, Marcus. It makes me think I can't trust you, and you're the one in control here. You realize that, don't you? You have the house, the money, everything in your hands. If you start lying to me..."

"I meant to tell you," I mutter. I rub my eyes and take a deep sigh, lean back against the post, stare at the ceiling fan that's turning in a lazy circle above us, barely stirring the air. "I didn't—I told myself I wouldn't and then I just couldn't help it, Kent. I'm weak against him. You're right, I need someone twenty-four seven, someone to hold me and touch me and kiss me, and when you wouldn't, then I couldn't stop myself—"

He holds up a hand to cut me off. "I don't want details," he says.

I duck my head, embarrassed. "Sorry."

For a long moment we're both lost in our own thoughts. *Two years,* I'm thinking, two years lost to this man, trying to make him love me, trying to convince myself he was someone I loved. I thought I knew him, but he just used sex to keep me here? I didn't even think he'd *think* of that, I have to admit it makes him stronger in my eyes, makes him almost calculating and sinister.

He likes the way I keep his house and his books, he knows I wanted attention so he gave me as much as he could to keep me interested. He doesn't love me...*he cares for me, though,* I tell myself, and there's that at least. If not love, then at least he felt *something* for me. And it was enough to piss him off when I told him about Luke.

Out in the market, someone calls for Kent, and we both turn to look at a woman and her husband by the register. She's waving frantically while her husband picks over tomatoes. "So now what?" I ask quietly.

Raising his voice, Kent calls out, "Coming!"

But he doesn't move. "Kent?" I prompt.

Instead of answering, he asks, "Where are you two headed?"

With a slight frown, I admit, "I don't know yet."

More silence. I'm about to mention my sister in California when he reaches into his pocket and draws out his wallet, battered leather held together with a rubber band. Opening it, he takes out a worn fifty dollar bill, folds it in half twice, and holds it out to me. When I don't move, he sort of shakes it at me. "Take it. For your help this week." With a nod at the screen door, as if he knows Luke is standing there listening in, he adds, "His too."

"Kent," I sigh and pinch the bridge of my nose between my thumb and forefinger, hard enough to make brightly colored dots dance behind my eyelids. "You don't have to do this."

He slips the bill between my fingers, forcing it into the palm of my hand. "Just take it already, will you? Take it and go."

As he passes me on his way to the steps, I catch his arm and wait until he looks at me to whisper, "Thanks."

He looks over his shoulder at Luke. "I seriously thought about asking you to stay," he tells me, shrugging my hand off of him. "I need someone here to help out with all the shit I don't want to do. But you lying...I can't have that, not if you're messing with my money and shit."

"I never," I assure him. "You know it."

He shrugs, like it's not really much to him one way or the other now. I guess it's not. "I can't trust you anymore," he tells me.

I know. I watch him cross the yard, his back so dark that it's almost burnt, his jeans hugging his ass and thighs, his cowboy hat cocked low over his eyes. From here he looks like everything I came out west to find, but he's not. Behind me, the screen door creaks open, slaps shut, and then warm hands find my waist, strong arms wrap around me, *this* is what I want, this boy holding me tight, Luke. I turn in his embrace and give him a sad smile. "So now what?" I ask.

Hugging me close, he buries his nose in my hair and says, "I told you, Marcus. I'm cool with whatever you want to do. Just don't leave me behind."

I lean back into him and savor the lips on my neck, the breath that tickles beneath the collar of my shirt. How can I give this up? "I told you I wouldn't," I murmur, turning to kiss his cheek. Down in the market, the customers seem to have multiplied, and Kent moves among them like a western hero, someone I once thought he was. "How far can fifty bucks take us?"

"I've got some money, too," Luke reminds me and I kiss him tenderly, I love kissing him. My hands smooth across his stomach—despite the early hour and all that's happened this morning, I want him already. "Where do you want to go?" he whispers against my mouth.

I've made my choice, there's only one answer to that question for me now. I tell Luke, "With you."

about the author

AN AUTHOR OF gay erotic and romantic fiction who began in self-publishing, J.M. Snyder recently started to work with electronic publishers such as Aspen Mountain Press, Amber Allure Press, and Torquere Press. Snyder's highly erotic short gay fiction has been published online at Ruthie's Club, Tit-Elation, and Amazon Shorts, as well as in anthologies published by Aspen Mountain Press, Cleis Press, and Alyson Books. A complete bibliography, as well as free fiction, book excerpts, purchasing information, and exclusive contests, can be found on the author's website at jmsnyder.net.

Because Snyder liked both Kent and Luke, for various reasons, *Cowboy* was originally serialized online and readers polled to determine who Marcus would choose at the end of the story. The full text is still available in e-book format as a free download on the author's website at jmsnyder.net.